e narrowed he

en married bef

'.'

I look stupid? She rec̶e̶i̶v̶e̶d̶ ̶his message loud and
̶ar.

ght.'

wrote 'COMMITMENT-PHOBIC' in her 'Getting
quainted' column. She believed in marriage when
people loved and trusted each other and were
mitted to making it work. She just didn't believe
she personally could do the long-term bit. Or
be she was afraid to believe.

that make her as commitment-phobic as him? she
dered momentarily. Not at all, she told herself. She
n't phobic, just…careful. Right?

also serious about sharing a little pleasure around
business aspect,' he said.

ell, maybe I'm not.' She added 'APPROACH AT
N PERIL' to the list and slapped her notepad shut.

u were enjoying it fine a few moments ago.'

eyes dared her to take issue with the inconvenient
th.

u didn't give me time to…to change my mind,' she
d of their kiss. 'I wasn't ready.'

u've been ready since the last time we bumped
s.'

acing his forearms on his knees, he gave her that
exy gr
couch

Anne Oliver was born in Adelaide, South Australia, with its beautiful hills, beaches and easy lifestyle. She's never left.

An avid reader of romance, Anne began creating her own paranormal and time travel adventures in 1998 before turning to contemporary romance. Then it happened—she was accepted by Harlequin Mills and Boon for their Modern Heat™ series in December 2005. Almost as exciting, her first two published novels won the Romance Writers of Australia's Romantic Book of the Year for 2007 and 2008. So, after nearly thirty years of yard duties and staff meetings, she gave up teaching to do what she loves most— writing full time.

Other interests include animal welfare and conservation, quilting, astronomy, all things Scottish, and eating anything she doesn't have to cook. She's travelled to Papua New Guinea, the west coast of America, Hong Kong, Malaysia, the UK and Holland.

Sharing her characters' journeys with readers all over the world is a privilege and a dream come true.

You can visit her website at www.anne-oliver.com

Recent titles by the same author:

THE PRICE OF FAME
THE MORNING AFTER THE WEDDING BEFORE
THERE'S SOMETHING ABOUT A REBEL

MARRIAGE
IN NAME ONLY?

BY
ANNE OLIVER

MILLS &
BOON

First published in Great B?????? ???2013
by Mills & Boon, an imprint of Harlequin (UK) Limited.
Harlequin (UK) Limited, Eton House, 18-24 Paradise Road,
Richmond, Surrey TW9 1SR

© Anne Oliver 2013

ISBN: 978 0 263 90002 6

Harlequin (UK) policy is to use papers that are natural, renewable and recyclable products and made from wood grown in sustainable forests. The logging and manufacturing process conform to the legal environmental regulations of the country of origin.

Printed and bound in Spain
by Blackprint CPI, Barcelona

MARRIAGE
IN NAME ONLY?

CHAPTER ONE

AT LEAST SHE was going to die in spectacular fashion.

Chloe Montgomery clenched her fingers around the tacky tar-smelling rope and tried to imagine that she wasn't suspended *who knew how high?* above the pitch-black auditorium in one of Melbourne's finest entertainment venues.

A rough knot below her feet scratched her bare soles. The way-too-small-barely-there costume dug into her ribs, making breathing almost impossible—especially when every shallow gasp could be her last.

'You'll be fine, Chloe,' the guy behind her whispered as he made a final adjustment to the slim safety harness at the back of her waist. 'Trust me, you'll be the highlight of the evening's entertainment.'

'Trust you…' Her voice came out reed-thin, a touch hysterical and barely audible above the rushing sound in her ears. How was she going to get one note of Happy Birthday out when her throat was closing over? She was no singer at the best of times.

'Ready?' the guy murmured.

'Mmm-hmm,' she managed between tightly pressed lips. What insane reasoning had convinced Chloe that she was up for this—in any way?

Because she wanted—*needed*—to prove to her new boss

that she was an asset to her event-planning business. No task too hard, no unforeseen circumstance she couldn't handle.

So when the artist booked for the event was involved in a car accident on the way here, Chloe had stepped up to the plate—or, in this case, the rope. And if everything went as planned, she'd be lowered onto the birthday boy's lap, kiss him on the cheek, someone would be there to unfasten her harness and she could escape to the venue's kitchens, challenge met and dignity intact. Dana would be only too grateful and impressed and desperately keen to take on such a valuable, *flexible* employee full-time.

A single spotlight exploded into life, blinding her with its brilliance and holding her captive in its hot white light. The audience's hushed murmur of anticipation rose into the stratosphere and she could feel every pair of eyes focused on her. Chloe, who'd spent her life trying and mostly failing to be someone people noticed, was finally the centre of attention.

A pity she was going to be remembered for all the wrong reasons.

Thought fled as the rope shuddered and began its descent. *You're supposed to sing,* she reminded herself. *Find the target, focus on him.* She squinted through the glare to the table directly beneath her. The cake, flickering with candles amongst champagne flutes, red foil stars and silver-ware, marked her destination.

A man was staring up at her with a faint smile—or was it a smirk?—on his lips. Hard to tell in the spotlight's dazzle but there was enough candle-glow to make out that they were, indeed, very nice lips. Forget the lips—*imagine him naked*—wasn't that what people afraid of public speaking were supposed to do? It couldn't hurt here either.

Except that his wife had organised this surprise. Which reminded her she had a job to do...

Clearing the constriction from her throat, she launched

into a wobbly, out-of tune rendition of Happy Birthday, keeping her eyes pinned to his as she descended. *Not* imagining him naked. Much.

Brilliant timing; she sang the last note as she reached table height and safety. She had to manoeuvre herself and the rope a little to ensure she landed on his lap. Her body prickled hot and cold all over when her barely covered bottom came into contact with a pair of rock-hard thighs, and she had to shift slightly to keep from falling off. Which would be easy to do because her whole body was trembling.

Warm palms slid firmly to her waist to steady her and she stifled a gasp at the electrifying contact. How embarrassing. How *wrong*. She lifted her chin and met his gaze. Up close his eyes were blue. A piercing, blinding blue that, to her shame, melted her insides to mush. 'Happy Birthday…' she finished in her best Marilyn Monroe voice, then came to a breathless pause. What the heck was his name again? Oh, my, he was…

Not available, Chloe.

She leaned in to brush the expected kiss over his cheek, caught the whiff of his enticing masculine skin before his head turned and his lips were somehow on hers. Warm, firm. Friendly. *Too friendly*. Appalled, she peeled her lips away to stare at him. He stared back, those fascinating blue orbs sending all the wrong signals for a married man.

'I'm not the birthday boy,' he told her, before she could blink. He leaned closer so that his breath tickled her ear and murmured, 'But then you already knew that, didn't you?'

Huh?

He jerked a thumb at the man on his left and leaned back, his hands dropping away from her waist. 'Sadiq's the one you should be kissing.' The tone of bored cynicism belied the heat in his eyes.

She felt the safety harness being unclipped and realised

she was *still sitting on his lap*. And…she went completely still…was she turning him on?

Not waiting to find out, she slid off immediately, her legs barely supporting her. 'Hey, *you* kissed *me*,' she whispered into his ear, keeping her smile in place, but furious with his dismissive attitude and furious with herself for making the mistake in the first place.

She turned her attention to the handsome black-haired, dark-eyed man who'd have looked right at home in one of those desert romance books. Way less unsettling. He was watching the two of them with an amused look, apparently unconcerned she'd stuffed up so sensationally.

'*Sadiq,*' she said with forced brightness and leaned down to kiss him to a roomful of enthusiastic applause. She wished him an enjoyable evening or some such but her mind was stuck on the previous thirty seconds.

You already knew. The weird—and incorrect—accusation burned like a hot wire in her blood. How dared he—whoever the hell he was—insinuate she'd contrived this act to some-how seduce him?

Sexual harassment. The taste of bile rose up her throat. An employee's word over some fancy schmuck with the wealthy connections? Like that was ever going to happen. One word of complaint from him and Dana was *so* going to fire her.

Jordan Blackstone watched the blonde's pretty cheeks flush, her well-endowed cleavage on full view as she made a fuss of his friend, privately enjoying her discomfort…and more than a little disconcerted at his own. Thankfully, she'd stood up before things had got too awkward. Another moment of her cute rhinestone-encrusted butt squirming on his lap, he'd have been in real trouble.

Women were always contriving new ways to meet him and he had to admit this one was unique. As was his body's response to hers. He hadn't expected to find his dormant libido awakening so fast and so hard.

He watched her drop a quick kiss on Sadiq's cheek. His own lips tingled at the memory of how they'd felt beneath his. *Soft and sweet.* What the hell had possessed him? Sheer momentary madness obviously, because in that pulse-pounding moment he sure as hell hadn't been himself.

She didn't hang around. He'd barely blinked and she was gone in a flash of sparkles and skin. The sort of shimmering flash that lingered on your retina long after the moment had passed.

He shook his head to clear the image. Soft and sweet was just a facade. No matter that she'd played the innocent mistake game, she was the type of out-there, attention-grabbing, rich-man-hungry woman he avoided. And that costume—what there was of it—was obviously intended to over-enhance her curves. Even if said curves were every man's fantasy, it was hardly appropriate for this occasion.

And she couldn't sing to save herself.

He picked up his glass, drained the bubbly mineral water to moisten his throat, which he realised had gone dust-dry, and watched Sadiq blow out his candles. A hovering waitress whisked the cake away to cut and distribute to the roomful of elite guests.

The band struck up a party number and dancers hit the polished floor amongst the bobbing helium balloons. Jordan gazed at the ceiling as the rope snaked upwards and disappeared over a balcony. 'Well. That was…interesting.'

Sadiq chuckled. 'Not as interesting as the look on your face when the lady landed on your lap, my friend. And that kiss… Want to tell me what you were thinking?'

Jordan scowled. 'I *wasn't* thinking.' And that was the problem. He had to be grateful for Sadiq's request to ban the media from inside the venue or he'd be front and centre in tomorrow's gossip rags.

His friend leaned closer and spoke over the noise. 'A discreet word here or there and you could get lucky tonight.'

'I make my own luck.' A sultry image involving him peeling that costume from her lithe and voluptuous body danced on his eyelids. He blinked it away. 'And she's hardly my type.'

Another chuckle. 'You have a type?'

Jordan didn't bother to reply, just reached for the water carafe and filled his glass. *Not his type?* Hell, certain parts of his anatomy obviously begged to differ. She was hot, no question. And wasn't that all he was looking for in a woman these days? Hot and single and temporary?

The sounds of merriment swirled around him as the music quickened, its throb beating low and heavy in his sensitised groin. He drained his glass, then tugged at his collar. Ever since she'd plonked that sexy butt on his lap and he'd felt her womanly assets graze his chest, his clothing had felt two sizes too tight. He could still smell her fragrance—warm and spicy and sensuous, making him think wicked thoughts; like lying naked with her in front of a roaring fire, her skin flushed with heat from their love-making.

Then there were the eyes. The colour of aged Scotch. He hadn't missed that initial flare of attraction, that quick clash of heat on heat, gone before he could think *hot night in paradise.* No, he hadn't misinterpreted that, but recognition…? He frowned. Had he got it wrong?

Because after the kiss and the accusation, those eyes had burned with a very different kind of heat—indignation. If there hadn't been an audience, he had a suspicion he'd have felt the hot sting of that anger in one way or another.

And now that he thought about it, quite possibly he'd have deserved it. Maybe she was already in a relationship? But she hadn't worn rings—and why he'd noticed was beyond him.

He relegated the confounding incident to the back of his mind, glanced at his watch and pushed up. Unfortunate timing, but his mate's thirtieth birthday bash clashed with important business. He clasped Sadiq's shoulder on his way. 'Gotta go. Teleconference with Dubai in an hour.'

His friend nodded. 'Good luck. You're still on for lunch tomorrow?'

'I'll be there.' He dropped a light kiss on Sadiq's wife's cheek. ''Night, Zahira. Great party. By the way, I loved your surprise.'

Zahira's dark exotic eyes smiled. 'Wasn't she delightful? And so brave to step in at literally a moment's notice.'

Jordan, who'd already turned to leave, swung back. 'Is that so?'

'The original artist had an accident earlier tonight,' she explained. 'A member of Dana's staff volunteered to take her place.'

Jordan felt a prick of guilt. Not a professional entertainer then, but a girl with maybe no experience who'd stepped in to save the day. That accounted for the debacle of a performance. It excused her actions; it didn't excuse his. 'Good for her,' he mumbled. Then because he admired people prepared to give it a go and he'd treated her less well than he might have, he said, 'She deserves a bonus at the end of the evening.'

Zahira flicked him one of those unreadable female looks. 'I'll tell her you said so when I hand it to her, shall I, Mr Blackstone?'

An odd sensation prickled the back of his neck. 'That's not necessary—I'll tell Dana tomorrow at lunch.' He pulled his car key from his pocket. 'Enjoy the rest of the evening.'

Except for her boss, Chloe was the last to leave the building when she exited through the staff entrance at two a.m. She pulled on the worn leather jacket she'd bought at a charity shop and swung her backpack onto her shoulders, glancing at the sky's heavy underbelly and hoping she could make it home before it rained. The birthday boy's wife, Zahira, had stopped by with praise aplenty and a nice fat wad of notes. *And* Dana had asked her if she wanted to take on regular work. Chloe did a little happy dance right there on the footpath.

What an evening! One minute she'd been swirling raspberry liqueur sauce over the desserts and wondering how she was going to make ends meet, and the next she'd been dangling over a balcony in a borrowed costume and singing in public.

Of course, it hadn't *all* gone according to plan. She'd got the wrong guy, after all. And Mr Wrong had *smirked* at her—she was sure of it. She'd be the first to admit she couldn't sing, *and* she was dead scared of heights, but she'd tried, hadn't she? Jerk.

Then he'd kissed her. Tingles shivered through her body at the memory. The drugging taste of those lips, the way he'd held her safe on his lap so she wouldn't fall, his musky masculine smell. Until he'd all but pushed her off with some ridiculous accusation that she knew him.

Double jerk.

Chloe dismissed him with a snarl, then jammed on her helmet and headed for her scooter parked a few metres away and looking all the more ancient in front of a shiny new maroon SUV. *Forget him.* The important thing was she'd come out on top. So it hadn't been the world's best performance; she'd made twice as much money in one night than she had since she'd stepped back on Australian soil a fortnight ago, and a regular job with reasonable pay would give her a realistic chance to resave the money she'd lost.

She slowed her steps, rubbed her arms against the chilly winter air. And then it just might be time to consider reconnecting with her family. A friend she'd made while overseas had lost her chance to reconcile with hers when an accident had taken both parents. Chloe didn't want to have the same regrets.

A sharp *meep* spiked the air and she glanced at the parked car as its lights blinked, then behind her at the sound of brisk footsteps. A man was approaching, a black overcoat over one shoulder. He was tall and broad with a lanky stride.

As he drew nearer the amber street light turned his shirt a white-gold and washed over his face so she could make out his features. Dark brows, firm jaw. Generous full lips even at this distance.

She stifled a gasp inside her helmet. She knew those lips. She knew how they felt, how they tasted. Her pulse took off on its own wild journey as she watched him cross the footpath, open the door. He glanced at her over the roof as he climbed into his car but didn't recognise her with her helmet on.

Was she just going to stand there and let him go without giving him a piece of her mind? No, she was *not*. She was beside his big bad wheels in seconds, stepping off the kerb in front of him, rounding the bonnet as the lights beamed on. 'Hey!' She rapped on the driver's window. 'Hey.'

The window lowered halfway. Now she could see the blue intensity of his eyes, the thick brows above them raised in concern. 'Are you okay?' he asked her. 'Do you need assistance?'

She lifted her visor and stared at him. Watched the blue in his eyes grow deep and focused as recognition sharpened his features. 'I'm fine,' she said, without giving him time to draw breath. 'No, actually I'm annoyed. You're arrogant and rude and I don't know why you'd think I'd know you or why on earth you'd think I'd want to come on to you. Who are you anyway? No—' She slashed a hand through the air. 'Don't tell me—I don't want to know.' And flipped her visor down.

She hadn't given him so much as a microsecond to open his mouth. Jordan leaned back in his seat and watched her walk—rather, *stalk*—to the decrepit-looking scooter in front of him. She was even smaller than he'd thought and dressed entirely in black leather now with a lumpy backpack on her shoulders. So… He'd got under her skin, had he? Was she itching all over with the memory of that kiss?

He damn well hoped so.

Because he hadn't been able to rid himself of the feel of her compact body against his. Because she'd distracted him during an important conference call. Because she'd made him forget his coat, which was why he was back here at two o'clock in the morning.

And she was going to give him an exceedingly restless night.

Her scooter sputtered into life and took off down the street in a cloud of fumes. He gave her—and himself—a minute, then pulled away from the kerb and headed for home.

A short time later, he caught sight of her again when he drew up behind her at a red traffic light. The lights changed and she zoomed off ahead, her hair streaming behind her from beneath the helmet. Dammit—he wanted a chance to apologise, preferably while running his hands through that silky gold.

And that was the thing; he didn't go for blondes—especially small mouthy blondes. He preferred his women tall and dark, poised and sophisticated. But he'd felt the tiny quivers running through her limbs, the surprising fit of her small body against his. The fury in her eyes, all the more eloquent for its silence.

An almost-grin tugged at his lips. Any other night he might

have enjoyed the challenge—a night to slake his lust with a nameless woman. A woman who didn't know him. A feisty woman who'd give as good as she got. He had a feeling the little surprise package riding ahead of him ticked all three boxes.

But his conference call to Dubai hadn't gone as well as he'd hoped and his fist tightened on the steering wheel. Yes, he could have done with a bloody good distraction.

Suddenly, without warning, she veered to the side of the street. By the time Jordan had pulled over and climbed out with the honourable intention of asking if she was okay, she was standing on the footpath, helmet in hand, windswept hair tangled around her face, expression stony. Her free hand was curled into a fist and tapping against her thigh. Music floated from an all-night jazz bar nearby. A light rain misted the air.

'So I can add stalker to my list.' She shuffled her feet on the concrete, drawing his attention to clumpy knee-high boots.

He raised his hands to shoulder height. 'I'm on my way home. Forgot my coat earlier.'

She rolled her eyes. 'R-i-ght.'

'Look, I—'

'No, *you* look, whoev—'

'Stop!' He jabbed the air with a finger. 'Give me a chance to open my mouth, will you?'

A beat of silence filled the air between them. 'Fine.' She huffed out a breath, her spine stiff, mouth tight. 'Say what you have to say and leave.'

'This is my usual route home. I am not following you. And I *will not* follow you.' He paused, hopeful. 'Unless you ask me to.'

She didn't reply but he imagined he saw the tiniest glimmer of that earlier heat in her eyes, instantly doused.

'Though I do have to ask,' he continued carefully, 'are

you sure it's safe for a woman to be riding that thing alone late at night?'

'I don't need a bodyguard.' She glanced skywards. 'And I'd like to make it home before I drown.'

'Think that's possible?' He glanced at the scooter. 'That's not the most reliable-looking transport I ever saw.'

'The Rolls is in for a service.' She flicked at her dampening hair as the rain thickened but there was a touch of humour around her mouth and her voice had lost some of its sting.

'My name's Jordan. Jordan Blackstone.'

She studied his face a moment. 'Should I have heard of you?'

'Dana knows me,' he said, then, 'I've had one hell of a night, and I know you have.' He gestured to the nearby bar. 'I'll buy you a nightcap. I think we could both use one.'

'I don't drink and drive on an empty stomach, 'specially when I'm tired.'

'Coffee, then.'

'Thanks, but no, thanks.' She turned towards her bike.

Something inside him snapped—he didn't want to be alone tonight. He didn't want to go home and think about his messy situation. And he wasn't used to women turning him down cold.

'Wait.' He reached out, his hand encircling her wrist, keeping his touch light, giving her a choice. Her eyes widened at the contact but she didn't pull away. The tip of her head barely reached his shoulders, arousing his protective instincts. 'Is anyone expecting you?'

She hesitated. 'No. But my housemates will know if I'm… late.'

'What's your name?'

'Chloe.'

'Chloe.' He smoothed his thumb over the delicate skin at

her wrist, felt her rapid pulse thrumming in time with his own. 'I want a chance to explain about earlier.'

She shook her head but left her hand in his, confusing him further. 'Why?' Dark eyes skewered into his. 'It wasn't as if it was memorable or anything.'

That brought a smile to his lips. 'You enjoyed it as much as I did.' He couldn't resist; he shifted closer, smelled leather and spice and warm woman.

She didn't back away and he heard the tiny hitch in her breath, saw the flare of heat in her eyes even as she said, 'You really are an arrogant piece of w—'

'Ring Dana. If anything happens...'

'Nothing's going to happen.' She withdrew her hand and pointed up the street. 'See that neon sign? I'm going to sit down in there in the nice bright *public* light where there are people and eat a burger.' Then she pulled on her helmet.

He watched her shapely black-clad legs, the curve of her backside as she climbed onto her scooter, and his groin hardened at the mental image of her astride *him*, thighs clenched around his hips, her head thrown back in passion as she tangled her fingers in her own hair and shouted his name. His blood simmered and smoked in his veins. *I could give you the ride of your life*.

She didn't so much as glance his way before she zoomed off. Which was probably a good thing.

But it was a clear invitation and he jumped into his car and followed. The evening might not end so badly after all.

CHAPTER TWO

JORDAN GAVE HER a few moments to order and waited until she'd taken up residence at a table before following her inside. She was munching on a burger by the time he sat down opposite her with his own and a side order of fries.

He slid a foam cup in front of her. 'I didn't know what you like. Most people like cappuccino.'

'Not at ridiculous o'clock in the morning if you want a decent night's sleep,' she said around a mouthful of bun. 'But thank you.'

'You're welcome.'

'So are you a movie star or something? On one of those Aussie soaps? I've been out of the country for eight years. I'm not up on the latest celebrities.'

Obviously fame didn't impress her, which made for a refreshing change. 'I'm in the mining industry.'

She studied him curiously. 'Why did you think I'd know you, then?'

He shrugged, wishing he'd never made the accusation in the first place. Except he wouldn't have been sitting here sharing burgers with her if he hadn't. 'The company's had some publicity over the past couple of years.' Which he didn't want to go into. 'What I said… What I did…' He was unwrapping his snack but paused. 'I apologise. I was out of line. And you're right, it was rude and arrogant.'

'Something we can agree on.' She arched a slim brow. 'Do you make a habit of kissing random women?'

'Only beautiful ones who fall into my lap at birthday parties. About that—I'm hoping we can do it again sometime.'

She blinked, her burger halfway to her mouth. 'My sixty seconds of fame. I'm not likely to be repeating that any time soon.'

But he knew *she* knew exactly what he meant. As he watched her cheeks turned pink, her eyes darkened and met his for a few unguarded seconds before she reached for her coffee. She took a sip, leaving a tempting fleck of foam on her upper lip.

'I didn't know you filled in at the last minute until Zahira told me,' he went on. 'That was a pretty game stunt you pulled. I'm ashamed to say, I'd have had second thoughts about the safety of that rope myself.'

'Yes, well, that's me. Always up for a challenge.' She licked the foam off with the tip of her tongue and said, 'Apology accepted, by the way. But that doesn't mean I'm going to let you follow me home.'

'You don't need to worry.' No matter how he'd have preferred to end the evening.

She nodded. 'Thanks.'

'Eight years is a long time to be away.' She only looked around twenty. 'How old were you when you left?'

'Nineteen. I'm an adventureholic, couldn't wait to leave.' She snaffled one of his fries. 'The freedom and independence. No one telling you what to do. No one to tell you you're doing it wrong.' Her voice turned sombre and the light faded from her eyes.

A man? he wondered. And things hadn't ended well. 'So what brought you back?' *Or chased you away.*

She chewed a moment, studying the table. When she looked up again, she was smiling, but she didn't fool him for a second. 'Family,' she said brightly, mask in place. 'You know how it is.' A haunted desperation flickered in her eyes before she looked away again, fingers tense around her bun.

Yes, he thought, those same emotions running through him, he knew how it was to owe family, but his bet was still on the man. He waited until she met his gaze once more then murmured, 'What did he do to you?'

Colour drained from her cheeks. 'Who?'

'The guy who put those clouds in your eyes.'

'I don't know what you're talking about—there's no *guy*, I was talking about my *family*.'

He nodded slowly. 'They're glad to have you back, then? Your family?'

'They live in Sydney.' Biting her bottom lip, she rewrapped the remains of her meal in record time, screwed it up and stood. 'I have to go.'

'Hang on.' He stood too. 'Can I see you again?'

'I don't think so.' She swung her backpack onto her shoulders, swiped up her helmet. Cool, guarded eyes met his. 'Thanks for the coffee.' Her tone was reasonable enough but the message was clear and final. A one-eighty-degree turnaround from the vibes he'd felt earlier in the evening when she'd swung down towards him.

Fine. He didn't need the complication in his life right now, anyway. 'You're welcome, and ride safely.'

He resumed his seat, studying her through the windows as she walked into the damp night, her blonde hair washed moon-pale beneath the car park's lighting. What was her story? She'd said she'd come back for family but hadn't caught up with them? She'd tripped over her tongue with that one and hadn't been able to get away from him fast enough.

Nope. She could deny it all she wanted—only a love gone wrong would elicit that lost-soul response he'd seen in her Scotch-coloured eyes.

And he ought to know.

His gaze lingered on her a moment more, then he turned away. She worked for Dana; she'd be easy to find. Tonight he had more important things on his mind than casual sex and other people's problems.

Such as how he was going to sweet-talk Sheikh Qasim bin Omar Al-Zeid into buying his gold.

Jordan's mother had inherited the majority shares in Rivergold when his father had died, and she'd nearly bankrupted the company—his father's love and life's work. Jordan had finally bought her out with the trust fund he'd inherited on his thirtieth birthday, but it had taken him two years of solid work and little sleep to bring it up to anything approaching its former glory.

His fingers automatically felt for the leather thong beneath his shirt. And he was back in time to eight years ago and he could see his dad lying on his office floor, barely breathing when Jordan had found him. He'd not been there in time because he'd been too busy heating up the sheets with a fellow student when his elderly father had demanded he come home to Perth to discuss his latest poor academic performance at one of Melbourne's finest unis.

He was the reason his father had died that day....

'Jordan...you came...' His old man's voice was barely audible.

He dropped to his knees beside his father, knowing it was already too late. 'I'm here, Dad, the ambulance is on its way. Just hang in there a few more moments and they'll be here and we can have that talk.'

'I don't have...that long...'

He barely raised a trembling hand, and Jordan grasped it, felt the thin, papery skin, saw the grey pallor of his lined face, the glazed eyes sunken into his skull. When had his dad grown so old? But seventy-nine *was* old. He should have known the bull of a man wouldn't last forever. *Jordan should have been here.* He *should* have made his father proud. 'Hang on, Dad, just hang on. Please.' *One more chance to show you I'm worthy.*

'Jordan, promise me…' Even through the pain he was fighting, the way he'd fought all his life.

Jordan leaned closer, heard the wheezing sound in his father's chest. 'What, Dad? Anything.'

'You'll inherit Rivergold one day. My dream, the gold… for you and your mother. Study hard, make Rivergold proud. Make me proud…'

He closed his eyes, the effort of talking taking its toll, and Jordan watched him fading away through misted eyes even as the wail of approaching sirens split the air. 'I promise. Dad, you'll—'

'My nugget. Wear it for me.'

Jordan looked at the irregular thimble-sized chunk of gold on its leather thong resting on his father's chest—the first gold he'd discovered while prospecting in the remote Western Australian outback.

'It's yours now, son. Rivergold needs you.' He spoke faster now, wanting to get it all out before the end. 'I want my… gold in a necklace…give your mother. Those negotiations in the UAE…so important to me…'

'I'll make it happen, Dad,' Jordan said, and meant it down to the last cell in his body.

'Tell Ina I love…'

Then he was gone, his empty shell a shadow of his former self.

The paramedics hadn't been able to revive him. If Jordan had been there earlier, as requested, he might have been able to get him help in time. The man might not have had a heart attack at all. If he'd been there.

* * *

Jordan gulped down the remains of his coffee, bitter-tasting now, and reflected on the evening's tele-conference. Qasim hadn't mentioned it, but Jordan had heard via a source close to Sadiq that the prestigious Dubai jewellery manufacturer billionaire was also considering X23 Mining. X23's owner, Don Hartson, was Jordan's most bitter rival. *And married to Jordan's mother.*

How was that for irony? Not that she'd been any kind of mother to Jordan. The woman had married Hartson five minutes after Dad's death. Which had left Jordan to draw the obvious conclusion—Ina Blackstone had been having an affair behind her elderly husband's back.

Too distracted by her glamorous new lifestyle with a younger man, she'd let the company slide over the next few years, and, with Jordan powerless to prevent it, those negotiations his father had set up had fallen through.

But the day he'd turned thirty he'd bought out her shares, taken control of the company and reaffirmed the promise he'd made to a dying man.

He'd spent the last two years modernising Rivergold, refusing to lay off staff, some of whom had given his father years of loyalty. It had been tough—still was—but he was now consolidating. Increasing his exports. With Sadiq's contacts in the UAE, Jordan had been able to turn his negotiations to the reputed City of Gold once again.

And now that long-ago promise he'd made to his father was so close he could almost reach out and kiss it.

But apparently the elderly gold manufacturer had a reputation for extreme conservatism. Blowing out a slow breath that seemed to take a part of him with it, Jordan stepped out of the restaurant and into the chill evening. He'd never been one to toe the line, but for this long overdue deal he'd do whatever it took.

CHAPTER THREE

CHLOE'S HEART SKIPPED a beat when she checked her phone for messages while dressing for Sunday brunch and saw an email from her sister. It wasn't tragic news, thank God, but it was disturbing news just the same.

Donna's message was brief and clear and to the point and included a bank account number. Their parents were facing tough times. Losing the family home was more than likely. And since neither her brother nor Donna could help out financially *at this time*—her sister outlined their perfectly valid reasons why they *couldn't* in bullet point format—they'd really appreciate Chloe's financial support since she had a high-paying job and lived in a virtual palace with a member of the aristocracy.

Stewart. Chloe beat back the pain with a sharp stick and thwacked that stick at the man she'd fallen in love with. The gorgeous hunk of widower who'd employed her to care for his son then used her for sex, except she'd been too naive and blinded by love to see it that way until it was too late.

Of course she'd told her family; she'd relished telling them about her successes, her career as a nanny, the palatial home in rural England. The man in her life.

And four years ago when it had all turned to crap, telling them she'd made a mistake and that she didn't fit into the world of the rich and famous and never would hadn't been on her list of priorities.

She flicked the email off, tossed her phone in her bag. She'd have to come clean and tell Donna the bad news, and she wasn't looking forward to it.

An hour later, she swiped sweaty palms down her best jeans then adjusted the belt over her thigh-length tunic and hoped she'd dressed appropriately. She'd caught public transport to avoid the dreaded windswept, helmet-hair look. Hitching her bag higher on her shoulder, she stared at the massive two-storey mansion as she walked up the long, curved drive. Dana's early-morning phone call had come out of the blue. Sadiq and his wife had extended an invitation to Chloe to attend an informal meal as a thank-you for helping to make last night's entertainment a success.

She'd been stoked. Dana's Events was one of the city's premier event-planning businesses, catering to the elite, and this was a brilliant opportunity for Chloe to get to know the clients.

The only downside was the probability that Jordan Blackstone would be there. And after the relentless dreams she'd had of the two of them last night… The residual heat was still stroking her abdomen, and her skin felt tight and tingly. Worse, she was mortally afraid he'd see it in her eyes. He was the type of man who could read women's minds. He'd read hers last night, hadn't he? She should never have stopped for that burger. A momentary weakness she would *not* be repeating no matter how attracted she was to him.

Rich and influential, like Stewart. Not the type of man she needed in her life—a lesson she'd learned the hard way. And there were limits to how much risk one should take, both personally and financially. She'd learned that lesson the hard way too.

A smartly uniformed staff member welcomed her at the

front door. Chloe followed her across a huge tiled foyer where a heavy chandelier threw rainbows over brass and honeyed wood, along a wide passage hung with a mix of Eastern and European art.

The aroma of barbecued meat and Asian cooking wafting from the garden met her nose as she walked through an airy glass atrium filled with tropical potted plants.

Zahira turned from the intimate group of guests as Chloe stepped outside. 'I'm so glad you could make it, Chloe,' she said in her lightly accented voice, her dark eyes smiling. 'Welcome. Here's our brave little entertainer from last night,' she announced, and had every head turning their way. 'Chloe Montgomery, a member of Dana's capable team.'

'Hi.' She smiled at the group in general but there was only one pair of eyes she saw. Jordan Blackstone's. Blue and even more intense in the winter sunshine. Startling against his tanned complexion and spiky dark hair, which riffled around his temples in the breeze.

No avoiding him, she thought, as he said something to the knot of people he was standing with and began walking towards her. Her pulse thrummed fast and her breathing quickened while she watched him approach.

Unlike the rest of the guests who wore casual, he was dressed for business. A suit and tie for a Sunday brunch? Still, she couldn't help but be impressed by the clean-cut corporate image. Hopefully he was on his way to forge some million-dollar deal with some other mining magnate and she could relax and *not* think about sharing Sunday brunch with him in an entirely more intimate way.

'Morning, Chloe.' His smile was polite, his tone precise, almost professional. Only his eyes betrayed the hint that he hadn't forgotten last night's kiss either.

'Jordan. Hello.' She felt her face warm and prayed her

expression didn't give away her inner turmoil. Her dreams, her restless night.

Not to mention the fact that she'd almost blurted out her most private personal problems at the diner.

Then Zahira smiled enigmatically and made some vague comment about leaving her in Jordan's capable hands—which had her body tingling anew—and walked away, leaving the two of them standing alone together in the middle of the lawn.

'Would you like a drink?' he asked, motioning a waiter who was at her side in three seconds flat.

'Soda water, please. I skipped breakfast. Running late,' she added, though why she felt she had to explain…

'You didn't sleep well?'

Was that humour in his voice? 'Slept like a baby, thanks for asking.'

'The coffee didn't keep you tossing and turning all night?'

Not the coffee. But she *knew* he already knew that and was relieved when the waiter returned with her glass of bubbles. 'I was tired—that usually does it.' She took a cooling sip of her water and deflected his attention from her hot cheeks with, 'Do you always dress so formally for a barbecue?'

'I have a meeting in the city later.'

'Hello.'

Chloe looked down at the sound of the young voice to see a small girl with dusky skin and long black hair looking up at her. 'Hello, there.'

'What's your name?' she asked, fiddling with a gold brooch pinned to her dress. 'My name's Tamara. It means date tree. Mummy's is Zahira and it means blossoming flower and Daddy's is Sadiq and it means trooful. Daddy says I should always tell the troof.'

Chloe glanced at Jordan and they exchanged a smile before she leaned down. 'Your daddy's right. And my name's Chloe.'

'What does Chloe mean?'

'I don't know. I'll have to find out, won't I?'

Tamara's inquisitive gaze flicked between them. 'Is Jordan your boyfriend?'

'No,' Chloe said, startled. 'We…don't know each other very well.'

'Not yet,' Jordan murmured, sending ripples of awareness down Chloe's spine. He didn't look at Chloe as he ruffled the small girl's hair. 'How's it going, Tams?'

'I'm five now,' she announced proudly, holding up her fingers. 'And I go to school so I'm allowed to help light the candles on my daddy's birthday cake later.'

Chloe nodded. 'I'll be sure to be watching.'

'I think your daddy has something for you,' Jordan said, jutting his chin in the direction of the barbecue.

Tamara followed his gaze. 'Yum, sausages. Bye.' She waved a hand, setting a dozen gold bangles jangling along her arm, her frilly party dress shimmering in the sun as she skipped across the lawn to her father.

'She's a cutie,' Chloe said, meeting Jordan's eyes, still unsettled by the boyfriend question but determined not to let him see. 'And obviously likes to be the centre of attention.'

'Reminds me of someone else last night.' His eyes twinkled at her.

Oh, no. Too awkward. She loved attention but singing to an audience in a costume two sizes too small? And worse, kissing the wrong man? She coughed out a laugh. 'Please, I'd rather forget.'

'Well, I, for one, am not likely to forget any time soon.' He watched her without speaking a moment. Not that she was looking at him now—she was smiling and giving a finger wave to Tamara, who was holding up her sausage like a trophy—but she could feel the heat of his gaze, bathing her like sunshine and not letting her forget either. 'You like kids,' he said.

'You kinda need to if you want to work as a nanny.'

'Guess so. That job kept you busy a good while, then?'

Eighteen wonderful months of being a nanny to Brad while falling hopelessly in love with his father... *Don't go there.* She forced herself to meet Jordan's eyes. 'Only until I had enough money to get me to the next port of call.'

A tiny line furrowed between his brows, as if he was weighing up the truth of what she'd said. 'So...what else did you do while you were overseas? The usual waitressing to fund the campervan to Europe?'

'I wanted more than that,' she went on quickly, relieved the nanny topic was over. 'I picked grapes in France, trekked Nepal, worked on a trail restoration project in the Grand Canyon. Won a wet T-shirt contest in Rome and lost my money in—' Appalled, she bit her lips together. *Please tell me I didn't just say that.* To a man she barely knew. A rich and successful man who'd never have been so careless where money was concerned. She couldn't even blame her runaway tongue on too much wine.

This was the *however many* time in less than twelve hours that she'd said too much to Jordan Blackstone. It was *none* of his business. She should blame him. It was his fault she wasn't thinking straight.

'You ran out of funds,' he finished for her.

'Ye— *No.*' She chewed on her lip then plastered a smile on her face. He probably thought she had a gambling problem or something. 'Family—I told you already. Last night.'

'So you did,' he said slowly, watching her through eyes that were far too perceptive. 'I wasn't sure.'

Now he probably thought she'd come back to sponge off her parents. If he only knew it was the other way round. She eyeballed him back. 'Money's not important to me. Never has been, never will be.'

He didn't believe her, she could tell. And okay, money

hadn't been important until now. She looked away from his unsettling assessment and watched the wait staff setting platters of salads and aromatic Eastern dishes on a long glass table.

When she saw the tray of steaming barbecued delights arrive at the table, Chloe moved fast. 'Looks like the food's ready,' she said over her shoulder as she walked away. 'I'm starved.'

Chloe used the buffet meal to mingle with the other guests under the covered pergola. She didn't speak with Jordan again, but as she chatted she knew where he was at any given time by the way the hairs on the back of her neck tingled as if they were mini antennae seeking a signal.

So when Tamara asked her to come and look at her new cubby house, Chloe was only too happy to escape.

The little hideaway stood a metre or so off the ground. It was a perfect replica of a gingerbread house, crammed with child-sized furniture, books and toys. Tamara had just settled on a cushion when she jumped up and scrambled to the door. 'I forgot my princess crown in my bedroom. Wait, okay?'

'Okay.'

Chloe watched the child skip off across the manicured lawns in her designer dress and shiny shoes with what had to be a fortune in Dubai gold glittering on her arm and blew out a sigh.

Obviously this child was loved, indulged, no struggle to be accepted by her doting parents. Was just wanting to be loved and accepted for who she was too much for Chloe to ask? She stared around at the cubby, luxurious enough to live in.

Okay, money had never been a priority, but right now she could do with a fraction of that wealth. Who knew where her parents might end up without the home they'd lived in for forty years?

And why should she care? Why should Chloe Montgomery, an accidental offspring who'd never fitted in, never lived up to their expectations and had escaped overseas the moment she was old enough, feel any sort of familial obligation?

She rubbed a dull ache that had taken up residence in her heart since Donna's email last night. Because they were family, bonded through blood—however fragile that connection was.

As fragile as life itself, Chloe thought, remembering how devastatingly final Ellen's loss had been. Ellen had argued with her family and left without a goodbye and life had been sweet and exciting. But a couple of months ago her parents' car had been swept away crossing a flooded river in rural Victoria. Chloe would never forget the despair in Ellen's eyes as they'd said goodbye to each other at Vancouver airport.

A couple of months later, Chloe had decided maybe it was time to come home, too, and re-establish some sort of connection, but she'd needed just a little more cash...

Tamara scrambled up the little steps and burst through the doorway with a sparkling crown on her head and a skateboard under one arm. 'Can you read me a story?'

Chloe loved telling stories—making up her own adventures where the heroine always won in the end. She'd been doing it since she was Tamara's age. 'I can do better than that,' she told her. 'I'll tell you one.'

'How did last night's conference call go?' Sadiq asked Jordan as they wandered away from the group.

'I was right—I need to be there in person.' He tightened his jaw, stared out over the garden. 'If I can talk to Qasim face to face, I know I can convince him. I've made an appointment to meet with him next week.' He turned to his friend. 'You understand the way things are done there. What's it going to take?'

'Stability. Focus. Commitment.'

'You know me—I'm all three.'

'Where business is concerned, I agree one hundred per cent, but in other aspects of your life…?' Sadiq shook his head. 'It doesn't help when you're frequently in the media spotlight with a different woman superglued to your arm every night of the week.'

'Women have never interfered with my business priorities. They—'

'And Qasim's not going to like the possible repercussions for his own business,' Sadiq continued over the top of Jordan. 'He's old school, set in his ways, and has always been of the opinion that married men are more likely to put in the effort. He builds his business deals around that.'

'And you agree with that reasoning?'

Sadiq shrugged, as if it were nothing. 'I was brought up that way. Marriages have been arranged around business for centuries. My own marriage was arranged when we were ten years old.' His gaze searched out his wife amongst the women. She looked their way at that moment and they exchanged an intimate smile.

And Jordan felt something that might have been envy. If he were the type to play happy families. He'd learned he wasn't the hard way. He shoved his hands in his trouser pockets. 'I'm living proof that he's wrong. What's more, I'm going to prove it to him.'

'If anyone can, it's you.' Sadiq nodded encouragement. 'Still, it wouldn't hurt to have an advantage.'

'Like what?'

'Why don't you speak to Dana, check out Chloe's references?' A speculative gleam flicked briefly in his mate's eyes. 'Couldn't hurt.'

Frowning, Jordan studied him more closely. 'What do—?'

'What are you two looking so serious about?' Zahira appeared as if summoned by the couple's earlier exchange of

glances and laid a hand on Sadiq's arm. 'This is no time for
business talk—we've got a home-made party cake coming
up. Tamara helped bake it and she's been looking forward to
lighting the candles for weeks.' She looked about. 'I haven't
seen her in a while. Do you know where she is?'

'I saw her heading in the direction of the cubby house with
Chloe in tow,' Jordan said. He'd been watching Chloe all afternoon; he'd known exactly where she was at any given moment. He immediately turned in that direction. 'You two go
ahead. I'll tell her she's been summoned.'

The little door was open and Tamara was still for once,
utterly focused. They were cross-legged on the floor, facing
each other, and Chloe was telling Tamara a story.

Jordan stilled too, equally intrigued, watching the way
Chloe's small, slender hands moved as she talked. Listening to the vitality in her voice. Her flyaway hair was too
messy for his taste, her eyes incongruously big in her small
pixie face. But she could spin an adventure story out of thin
air and make it sound believable. She could charm any age
group. She could conquer high balconies and risky ropes at
a moment's notice...

An impossible idea was coalescing at the back of his mind.
Now the flicker of expression in Sadiq's eyes made some sort
of sense. Didn't it?

Attraction aside, she wasn't the usual acquiescent kind of
woman he dated, just as he very much doubted he was her
type of guy—if she had a type. According to her, she didn't
stay long in any one place so she'd probably never formed
any close attachments. And that had to be an advantage because they could walk away at the end, no complications...

He smiled to himself. Not such an impossible idea. Chloe
Montgomery might just be the up-for-anything kind of girl
he needed.

CHAPTER FOUR

'...AND THE PRINCESS—'

'Princess *Chloe*,' Tamara corrected.

'Not Princess Tamara?'

'It has to be Chloe 'cos it's your story,' Tamara said, then took her crown off, reached across and set it on Chloe's head. 'And you have to wear this.'

'Oh. Thank you.'

Jordan relaxed against the cubby's frame even as his mind raced ahead with possibilities and potential problems.

'Okay, Princess *Chloe* wanted to learn to skateboard—'

'A pink skateboard. With sparkles.'

'Exactly.' She nodded. 'But her father the king wouldn't let her.'

'Why not?'

'Because he didn't understand his daughter. He thought she should be learning to do princessy things like practising her curtsey and learning how to wave. And he wanted her to be safe.

'So Princess Chloe left a note—so the king and queen wouldn't worry—and ran away from the palace. She sold her crown so she could buy food and journeyed to the far side of the kingdom with her sparkly skateboard to find someone who could teach her. She wanted people to like her because she was clever, not just because she was a princess.

'She was away for a long, long time,' Chloe continued. 'She knew that the king and queen would worry so she sent messages with the birds about what she was doing. She told them about the man she met who could spin straw into gold—'

'Like in Rumpelstiltskin?'

'Yes. And that she lived in a shining crystal tower. But when she fell out of the tower and had to live in the forest again she didn't tell them.'

'She didn't tell the troof?'

'No, Tamara, she didn't. And that was a very bad thing because one day a wicked witch came and took all the gold and the palace away from the king and queen and made them sleep in the stables with the horses. Princess Chloe found out and wanted to help.'

He wasn't hiding—still, Jordan felt as if he was eavesdropping on someone's private confession, but he couldn't tear himself away. Nor could he bring himself to interrupt Chloe's story to tell Tamara she was required for candle-lighting duties. Because the longer he listened, the more intrigued he became. Some gut instinct was telling him this was no ordinary fairy tale.

He watched her lean close to the child, blonde to brunette. 'She went home because they were her parents and she loved them and one day they'd get old and d— She'd miss them. On the way she met a handsome prince.'

Tamara nodded, approval sparkling in her eyes. 'Ooh, a *prince*.'

'He promised to help her find some real gold if she'd give him her skateboard. And she was so happy because now she could go home and take the palace back from the wicked witch and they could all live happily ever after.'

'With the prince too?'

'Ah, but he *wasn't* a prince, Tamara. He was an evil sorcerer in disguise. He turned her skateboard into a yucky slimy log.'

'Uh-oh...' Tamara clapped her hands to her cheeks in true drama mode. 'He didn't give her the gold?'

'No, he didn't. He put on his special invisible cloak and Princess Chloe didn't know where he'd gone...'

Chloe trailed off, suddenly aware that the light from the doorway had dimmed, and that they were no longer alone. Uncomfortable heat flooded her cheeks. She turned to see Jordan, one shoulder leaning on the doorjamb, hands in his tailor-made trouser pockets, his expensive-looking silk tie flapping in the breeze.

With his height and the cubby's elevation, his face was in her direct line of vision and he was making no secret of watching her. Or listening in. And judging by his preoccupied expression, he'd been there for some time. Thinking.

Thinking what? It had been too easy to put too much of herself into the story—a familiar habit, but not one she shared with others. Sweat sprang to her palms and she swiped them down the front of her jeans.

'What happened then?' Tamara demanded.

Jordan pushed away from the door. 'Tams, Mummy's looking for you. It's nearly time to light the candles.'

'Now?' She pursed her lips. 'But Chloe hasn't finished her story.'

'Tell you what,' Chloe said, while her mind whirled. 'Why don't *you* be the storyteller? Think about how it ends and tell me later.'

Tamara nodded. 'Okay. I've got to light the candles now.' She shot up off her cushion and ran to the door, launching herself at the man. 'Lift me down, Jordan.'

He swung her down with a chuckle. 'There you go.'

Which left Chloe alone in a cubby with no place to hide.

Not for long though because somehow Jordan squeezed through the doorway and took Tamara's place on the cushion.

He looked so incongruous against the mini furnishings, dominating the tiny space with his size, his masculine scent, his charisma. Under different circumstances, Chloe might have laughed. Or leaned in and got reacquainted with those lips. Instead, she sucked in air that suddenly seemed in short supply. 'What are you doing? The cake...'

'We've got a moment. They won't miss us.' He stared at her hair. 'It looks good on you, *Princess Chloe*.'

'What?' Oh. She pulled off Tamara's crown, set it aside, her laugh coming out hoarse and strained and fake. 'I love kids' stories, don't you? Kids' games are so much fun,' she rattled ahead as she pushed up onto her knees. 'I promised Tamara I'd watch—'

'She's got herself in a bit of a tight spot—the princess.'

The way he said it... *How much did he know?* Her heart skipped a beat. 'Yeah, but she's independent and clever, she'll find a way out. She'll win.' The game, the gold, the guy, it didn't matter. Right now, Chloe would settle for the gold.

'She should find herself a real prince and marry him,' Jordan said. 'Isn't that how the story should end?'

'Ah, but does she want to marry this real prince? He's not like her and she hardly knows him. Maybe he'll turn out to be the evil sorcerer's apprentice...'

'Or maybe he can help. Chloe.' He reached out, encircled her wrist with a warm hand. 'Stories aside, maybe *I* can help.'

'What do you mean? I don't need help—yours or anyone's.' She tried to pull her hand away but his grip firmed.

'I think you do.'

'Who are you to think what I need?' She lifted her chin and glared at him. 'Anyway, I don't know what you're talking about.'

'Come on, Chloe. You've spun enough fantasy for me to draw some very real conclusions. You're short on cash.'

He released her and she sank back down, clasping her hands around her knees and feeling like a deflated balloon. 'You should have made your presence known.'

'I wasn't hiding. You were too involved in your story to notice. Can we talk about this?'

'What's to talk about? I already told you, I don't need anything. Or anyone.'

'Give me a minute here, Chloe. I'm considering making you an offer I'd like you to think about.'

She regarded him warily. 'What kind of offer?'

'A partnership. A business partnership. With no risk on your part.'

'Well, *that* sounds risky for a start.' He continued watching her without speaking for a moment until her curiosity got the better of her. 'Why would you want to help me? You barely know me.'

'I reckon we can help each other,' he said slowly. 'You need money, right?' When she didn't answer, he continued. 'You're adventurous, you say you're up for a challenge, you enjoy travel. That makes you the right kind of girl to make what I have in mind work.' His gaze slid to her mouth. 'The fact that I'm attracted to you has nothing to do with it.'

She refused to melt into a mindless puddle of lust at the way his last huskily spoken words slid through her insides like sun-warmed treacle. 'You kissed me last night to make me feel bad.'

He lifted his darkening gaze to her eyes and the puddle grew to a lake. 'The next time I kiss you, I can promise you, you won't feel bad.'

She pressed her lips together to stop the sudden rush of blood there at the thought of an encore. She didn't doubt he was up to the task. If she let him. Which, she told herself, she didn't have a mind to, no matter how prettily he promised. He *had* made her feel bad with his arrogant assumption that she knew him. 'You didn't mention anything about kissing. You said business.'

His mouth twitched and what looked like humour danced in his eyes. 'So I did.'

She shut off all thoughts of carnal pleasure. 'Business is hardly my forte.'

He leaned closer so that all she could see was him. All she could smell was his musky scent. 'It doesn't need to be—it's mine. But I want to think on it before I decide, so I'd like you to have dinner with me tomorrow night. We could get better acquainted.'

His voice made her think of a still river with hidden depths. And something in his expression, something she recognised because she knew that feeling of desperation too, drew her interest. He pressed his advantage. 'How does seven p.m. suit you?'

She studied him a moment. The way his eyes changed from cobalt to denim to azure depending on the mood and the moment. The clean-shaven jaw that smelled pleasantly of some exotic aftershave, the modern spiky cut to his dark hair, the precise fit of his perfectly tailored clothes.

An evening out with a gorgeous guy—why not? And that was all it would be. 'Dinner, then.'

The following day Chloe worked a busy corporate luncheon, which didn't leave her time to think about the evening ahead or to quiz Dana about Jordan in a busy kitchen—except to learn that he was a long-standing friend and an absolute 'darling'. *Uh-huh.* No men Chloe knew had ever deserved that rep so she'd reserve judgement on that.

She made it back to the semi-detached house she shared

with a couple of flight attendants fifteen minutes before Jordan was due to pick her up.

And yes, he'd made it clear before he'd left for his meeting in the city yesterday afternoon that he intended picking her up, and in the end she'd given him her address and they'd swapped phone numbers. It was a given he'd have her references checked out with Dana before he offered whatever business partnership he had in mind.

Fine. She had glowing reports from her overseas employers. Nothing to hide. Unless... She shook her head determinedly. Almost impossible to trace—unless he was looking for a nanny. She'd been innocent, used. Betrayed.

Chloe threw on her seasons-old black dress of soft wool and pulled on matching leather boots while she searched for her clutch bag. She refreshed her make-up and ran a brush through her hair, deciding his gentlemanly insistence was appreciated in this instance.

Her quick search last night had revealed that Jordan Blackstone owned a gold mine in Western Australia. He was involved in some charity called Rapper One and, according to a recent magazine poll, was one of the country's most eligible bachelors. His love interests were plenty and varied and colourful, not to mention stunning and sophisticated, but it seemed there was nothing remotely dodgy about the man's business reputation.

And nothing remote about her body's response when she answered the knock on her door either. Yet another dark suit, expertly fitted and accentuating his broad shoulders, but tonight he wore a black shirt and tie, giving him a temptingly devilish air. Even his eyes looked black in the hallway's dim light.

'Hi,' she murmured in a breathy voice she hardly recognised. She felt herself sway towards his enticing scent and gripped the door handle tight to stop from grabbing his lapels and launching herself at him.

'Evening, Chloe.'

His smile… A sigh rose up her throat and her knees went weak. Had she forgotten the effect those lips had on her? 'Hang on…' *Water.* She dashed back to the kitchen and filled a glass, gulped it down.

She smoothed her dress, took a deep breath, then marched down the hall, her boots echoing briskly on the worn wood in time with the words in her head. *I am not going to fall for good looks and charm ever again.*

He was leaning against the doorjamb but straightened as she approached. His smile had worn off and he looked concerned, as if she might have changed her mind. 'Are you ready?'

'As I'll ever be.' She pulled the door shut behind them.

He gestured to his shiny car parked at the kerb. 'After you.'

She spent the short journey to the city on a razor's edge beside him, so flustered she couldn't remember what they talked about besides her busy day, yesterday's brunch. Melbourne's traffic.

The up-scale French restaurant was glamorous but intimate with cosy candle-lit alcoves. *'Bon soir, monsieur, mademoiselle.'* A polished waiter showed them to their private corner table, fussed over their napkins and poured water into glittering glasses. Jordan asked Chloe's wine preference, then ordered expensive champagne, which arrived almost before she'd finished speaking. The wine was poured, the bubbles fizzed. Lights danced over crystal and silver.

In the corner, a lone musician in a felt beret squeezed early-twentieth-century French tears out of a piano accordion, the soft sound reminding Chloe of a favourite brasserie in the heart of Paris.

Jordan raised his glass. 'To a successful evening.'

'*Bon appétit.*' She clinked her glass with his. The cold liquid tickled her throat on the way down.

'What do you fancy?' he asked, putting his glass down and reaching for his menu.

Was that a trick question?

But he showed no sign of meaning anything other than food, and, pushing erotic images from her mind, she cast her eyes quickly to the menu in front of her. *Concentrate on your* stomach, *Chloe.*

When they'd decided on their choices, Jordan signalled the waiter. '*Nous voudrions l'assiette des fruits et fondue de Brie pour les deux, s'il vous plaît. Pour le plat principal, mademoiselle voudrait le filet de saumon au beurre rouge et je voudrais l'entrecôte è la bordelaise.*' He placed the menu on the table. '*Merci.*'

The waiter inclined his head. '*Merci, Monsieur.*'

Chloe spoke French well enough but listening to Jordan speak it was like having the back of her neck stroked with rich velvet. She indulged in the sensation a moment before forcing her thoughts back to the reason she was eating expensive French cuisine without prices in the first place.

'So what's the deal here?'

He rotated the base of his wineglass on the cloth and met her eyes. 'I spoke with Dana today. With your references and what I've learned about you so far, I'm satisfied you're the best woman for the job.'

'Oh? And what if I don't want this *job*?'

'You will,' he said smoothly.

She took a sip of wine and studied him over the crystal rim. 'So confident?'

'I'm always confident.' He leaned forward slightly. 'For the record, though, how badly do you need cash, and just as important, why?'

She hesitated, then decided what the hell? She had nothing

to lose and maybe something to gain. 'My sister emailed me that my parents could lose the family home. They always put us kids first, sent us to the best schools and paid our tuition fees because they hadn't had the opportunity themselves and wanted it for us. I was the only one who disappointed them and now they're elderly. Donna expects me...'

They'd not been in touch for years except for birthdays and Christmas and Chloe had never got around to telling them about her humiliating breakup. 'I want to help.'

He nodded. 'Sounds reasonable. And I need someone to help me win a lucrative contract overseas. Which makes it perfect.'

'Huh?' She stared at him, incredulous. 'How can a woman with no business expertise possibly help you win an overseas contract?'

His voice was polished business professional. 'You'd accompany me to Dubai as my wife.'

Her mouth dropped open. 'Excuse me?'

'In return for a very large sum of money.'

In the ensuing silence she clamped her hands to her head to keep it from spinning away. 'How large?' she said, finally. Faintly.

She thought she saw a smile of satisfaction flicker at the corner of his mouth, then he named a figure that had her head spinning in the other direction. And it wasn't just the money; everything about this proposal had *dangerous* plastered all over it.

'You like to play games, Chloe, so let's play Mr and Mrs Jordan Blackstone for a couple of weeks.'

She almost choked on an invisible lump in her throat and all she could think was, 'Why?'

'Say yes and I'll explain.'

She shook her head. 'It's ridiculous. Impossible.'

'You're already married?'

'No. I just…can't up and go away with you.' *But that kind of money*, a tiny, desperate voice whispered. 'Dubai…?'

'Have you been there?'

'No.'

'But that adventurous girl would like to, right?' He nodded. 'Think about it, Chloe.'

Oh, she was. She surely was. Like how easy it would be to fall into another man's honeyed money trap.

'If you're worried about publicity, no one need know,' he assured her in a soothing tone.

'Oh, yeah? The media obviously loves you. What if they see us together and get snap happy?'

'I'll make sure they don't. I'm an expert at not being seen when I don't want to be seen.'

Ideas were tumbling inside her head. She was already calculating what she could do with that kind of money. First and foremost she could ensure her parents kept their home, with plenty left over. For once in her life she'd be the golden girl. This man could be the fabulous guy she'd told her parents about. *Win-win*.

She shook her head. Forget fabulous guy. *What* was she thinking? This man wasn't Stewart, nor was he ever going to meet her family. 'I only just met you. I may be a risk-taker but I'm not stupid.'

'No, you're not stupid—you're being cautious. We can discuss it, then—'

'Discuss it…'

His lucrative business contract.

A fortune in cash.

A fake marriage.

'Why would a wealthy, good-looking guy such as yourself consider such a drastic course of action with short, plain-speaking, plain-dressing Chloe Montgomery, I'd like to know? Surely you have plenty of willing candidates?'

'Don't put yourself down, Chloe, and others won't.' His blue eyes mesmerised her. 'I'm sure willing candidates abound, yes, but I pride myself on reading people. I need a woman with particular qualities and you tick all the boxes.'

She felt a strange warmth flow through her veins, as if he was paying her a compliment even though he hadn't resorted to the usual complimentary—and often empty—words. However, she said, 'I'm not going into this without all the facts I need to make an informed decision.'

He nodded. 'I have questions too.' He leaned forward, his eyes intense. 'Let's be absolutely clear here. This is a business arrangement. We'll both sign an agreement to that effect. If you decide not to go ahead, I ask that you keep what I'm about to say confidential. Are we agreed?'

'Okay.'

He talked to her about Rivergold Mining and honouring his father's last wishes. By the time he'd finished, their starters had arrived. The fact that he seemed to be upfront with no hidden agenda was reassuring.

Still… 'How long would this "marriage" thing have to last?'

'Just until the business deal's agreed on and we come home.'

She chewed on her lips a moment. 'I want the money up front.'

He regarded her steadily a moment, then withdrew a legal-looking document. 'Read this fully, sign both copies and I'll deposit half the agreed sum in your bank account. The rest will be deposited as soon as the deal's done.'

'You *were* confident,' she murmured, almost afraid to think about how carefully he'd planned this.

'I had my lawyer draw it up this afternoon,' he said as she skimmed the first page. 'If you'd like your lawyer to check it over—'

'I don't *have* a lawyer,' she stated, then tapped the paper—
savvy business girl now. 'I want that first payment in my account *before* I sign.'

He shook his head. 'That's a substantial sum of money.
You're not the only one being cautious here.' He spooned
salad onto her plate beside the Brie tartlet. 'What would set
your mind at ease?'

'I'm not sure anything will. And I'll tell you why.' She cut
off a mouthful of the tempting tart in front of her. 'I trusted
a man,' she began. 'He was a lot like you.'

'In what way?'

'The kind of guy women can't resist.'

One eyebrow lifted as he pulled his dinner roll apart.
'You've resisted *me*. Quite admirably, I'd say.'

She felt a smile touch her lips. 'You don't want to know
what I was thinking when I opened my front door earlier.'

His gaze clashed with hers and heat met heat across the
table. 'If it was anything like what I was thinking, we're going
to get along very well.'

An image of them plastered together against her front
door, bodies slick with sweat, sent heat rippling like teasing
fingers through her lower regions. She almost moaned aloud
and her cheeks flushed and she reached for her water. They
had more to discuss here than the business arrangements.
'Umm…where was I?'

His eyes flirted, *Wherever it is, I'd like to be there with
you*, but, 'Mr Irresistible…' was what he said.

'Ah, yeah. Markos. Call him Mr Despicable.' She cast her
mind back to a time not so long ago. A time she'd rather forget
but one she needed to remember, particularly given tonight's
circumstances and the mission in front of her if she chose to
accept. 'A friend's family died in tragic circumstances while
she was overseas and it made me think about how long I've

been gone… I had some money saved up but I wanted to be able to have enough to show them I'd been successful…'

He watched her without speaking, and neither did she as the mains arrived and the waiter refilled their glasses.

'Why?' he asked when they were alone again.

'My family judges success by how many letters you have after your name and your well-paid *professional* career. I judge success by happiness and how you live your life. It's never been about money for me.'

'And they just didn't get you.'

But he did, she thought, relieved. 'No. Maybe I was home-sick after what happened with Ellen's family and I just wanted to be the person they want me to be for once.'

He drank some champagne, then said, 'Back to Mr Despicable…'

She forked up some of the flaked salmon. 'You heard my story yesterday.' She'd been so stupid, so naive. '"Prince" Markos turned out to be an evil sorcerer. The princess needed money and he was an acquaintance.

'He offered her an investment that promised a quick return. He tricked the princess into parting with what little cash she had, then disappeared. I had barely enough to get me home, let alone a job or accommodation…' *Trust me, Chloe.*

'And you haven't told your family you're back yet.'

She shook her head. *This* man, however—rather, his *offer*—would change her life. Her boss trusted him so she was prepared to take the risk. The only way from here was up, right?

Chloe pushed her half-finished plate to one side, reached for the documents and slid them in front of her. The terms were mostly straightforward. She looked up, met his eyes. 'This clause here…'

'…is saying I won't force myself on you. And the consequences if I did.'

He leaned in so that all she could see were his eyes. No bedroom heat in those brilliant blues right now but they were clear and honest and reassuring.

'What we have is a business arrangement,' he reiterated quietly. 'We'll need to share a room and act like newlyweds up to a point, bearing in mind that in Dubai public displays of affection are unacceptable. But trust me, Chloe Montgomery, winning this contract is worth more to me than—'

Sex. 'You don't need to spell it out, Mr Blackstone. I understand clearly.' *And a golden fortune in compensation if he breaks it.*

So why did his matter-of-fact reassurance that she wasn't at the top of his 'to-do' list somehow disappoint her? 'For the record, if we were to…' She trailed off, flustered as heat bled into her cheeks.

His eyes darkened. 'Take things further?' The way he said it, all smooth and chocolaty. After-dinner delights…

'Forget it.' Chloe pushed the words out before he could respond, digging into her bag and pulling out a pen. Did she sound desperate and dateless or what? She scribbled her signature on both copies, pushed them back to him without looking at him.

Of course abstinence would be the wisest decision, she told herself, studying her hands on the tablecloth. She wasn't a woman who shied away from a man she found attractive, but getting involved on an intimate level with a man she was entering into a business partnership with was fraught with all kinds of danger. Even if that partnership was a faked marriage.

Especially if it was a faked marriage…

Jordan signed too, then tapped into his smartphone. 'Do you have your bank details handy?'

CHAPTER FIVE

WHILE HE STIRRED the froth on his coffee, Jordan watched the girl who'd agreed to help for any sign of how she was feeling. No visible emotion. She was scrolling through her phone options as if he didn't exist. Checking her account balance? International flight schedules to Ibiza or Acapulco? She hadn't so much as glanced at him since she'd signed the documents.

A fleeting self-doubt wrapped around his gut. What was stopping her from doing a moonlight flit with his money tonight? He'd learned not to trust so easily a long time ago, especially where women were concerned; they could literally take off at a moment's notice. And the enormity of this gamble was taking on the proportions of the Hindenburg, with the same potential for disaster.

For God's sake, stop second-guessing yourself. He might have just met her but he knew Chloe was no Lynette.

All that aside, he needed to get them both to Dubai ASAP. He also wanted to keep her with him 24/7 until the deal was done, but he knew that wasn't likely. And he didn't want to spook her by being too full-on and risk the deal going wrong.

On the other hand, she'd told him money wasn't a motivator, and, from the expression in her eyes when she'd said it, he believed her. He'd seen firsthand that she was the sort who was willing to step in and help out in a pinch—for her employer and her family…and Jordan too.

Trust issues aside, it was blatantly obvious she was as attracted to him as he was her and he was hoping they might mix a little pleasure with their business. There was nothing in the agreement to prevent that, provided both parties were willing. He reached for his own mobile. 'We should get some details out of the way tonight.'

'Hmm…'

'Do you have any commitments over the next few weeks?'

She finally looked up from her phone. 'Dana's just given me full-time work, so, yes, I do.'

'Apart from that.' He sent Roma, his PA in Perth, an email confirming his schedule. 'Can you be ready to leave tomorrow?'

It didn't sound like a question and she blinked. 'You're kidding, right? I just told you, I've got a new job. I'm trying to be responsible.'

'That's very commendable, but I'm paying you to be responsible with *me*. Our business has priority over everything else. That includes your social life, by the way.'

She raised a brow. 'It's fortunate then that I have no upcoming social events on my personal calendar, isn't it?'

He frowned. He didn't know why he'd made that brusque demand. Except that he didn't want anything or anyone interfering with his plans, which included having Chloe exclusively to himself for the next week or two. He was confident it wasn't going to be all work and no play. 'I'll make sure Dana holds your position,' he said more reasonably. 'That's if you still want it when we come back.'

'Of course I'll want it.'

Her quick and definite response surprised him. It wasn't exactly a highly paid sought-after career move they were talking about.

'I don't have any paper qualifications so I'm limited in choices,' she said, as if reading his thoughts. 'I never studied.'

He caught a wistfulness in her tone. 'You'd have liked to?'

'Yeah. Maybe counselling.' A wry smile tipped one corner of her mouth. 'Even if it's just to understand myself better. And you need to be settled in one place and I don't know if I can after all this time. Staying power, perseverance and tenacity are not my strengths.'

'But in a couple of weeks you'll have the money to make it happen.'

'Yes,' she said, almost as if startled by the revelation. 'I suppose I will. I've never had my own money—not *money* money. And this is like…wow…'

Her dreamy expression lingered as if she was already wishing herself far far away. *Staying power wasn't one of her strengths.* 'Very well, you've got tomorrow to get organised.' While he finalised travel arrangements and his business plan with Qasim. He signalled the waiter for the bill.

'Hang on…' She cleared her phone's screen. 'We're not going home already, surely? We don't know nearly enough about each other yet. Or how to do this…thing…'

Exactly.

He nodded. 'It could take a while.' *This thing* needed careful consideration and exploration. 'It could take all night.' His voice suddenly sounded lower than his belt buckle—which was no surprise given where his thoughts were leading—and Chloe noticed too because she looked at him sharply, those whisky eyes splashed with awareness.

'To make plans,' he clarified, not taking his gaze off hers.

'And get better acquainted,' she agreed, staring back and shifting forward in her chair. A hint of inviting cleavage caught his attention as she rested her forearms on the table ready to begin.

He liked the prospect of getting better acquainted. A lot. He leaned closer so he could smell that scent of cinnamon, citrus and jasmine that was fast becoming one of his favourites. 'We'll be more comfortable at home. We could go to my apartment, but yours is closer. Is it okay if we go there?'

'I only have a single bed…' She gave a little hiccup and shook her head, looking dismayed. 'Omigod. Did I say that aloud? That's not what I meant.' Pause while she blinked at him. 'Is that what *you* meant? Not that I was thinking about bed—not in that way. Because this is a *business* arrangement. I get that. We need to talk. I need to pack. I probably won't have time to sleep at all—'

'Chloe.' He kept his smile on the inside. 'Take a deep breath.'

She stared at him another beat, then closed those panicked eyes and sucked in air deeply. Exhaled in one long slow stream.

He took the opportunity for a leisurely all-out perusal of her face and he couldn't decide which he wanted to kiss more—her pulse doing star jumps at the base of her throat, or the scattering of freckles across her nose. After reacquainting himself with those plump, pouty lips, that was.

When she opened her eyes again, she seemed to have regained some composure, but she wasn't looking at him, she was staring at the tablecloth. 'I tend to go on when I'm stressed or excited or…plotting fake marriages.' She blew out a strangled-sounding breath, dropped her phone into her purse. 'Let's just get out of here.'

What had she done?

Chloe chewed her lower lip as Jordan pulled up outside her place. Suggesting getting better acquainted in that smoky, siren's voice she'd never heard coming out of her mouth before?

Then the bit about her single bed had literally popped out. She stifled a groan. *Because* he'd been talking about how it might take all night and being more comfortable and…and looking at her as if he wanted to devour her at the earliest opportunity, and her focus on the trip had got muddled up with a sexual fantasy and *how was she going to keep things strictly business?*

She'd never had a problem compartmentalising the men in her life. With one past regrettable exception, it was either business or pleasure—simple and uncomplicated. Her male acquaintances either fitted in one or the other.

Until Jordan.

He switched off the engine. Silence and anticipation thickened the air. Not hanging around to see if he'd try a squeeze or a kiss; she was already out and halfway up the path when she heard Jordan's car door shut and the alarm's *meep*. Her shoes tapped a staccato on the pavement, oddly loud and a tad desperate in the quiet suburban evening.

The scent of damp leaves and smoky log fires gave way to old wood and last night's reheated tandoori chicken as she pushed open the front door—the front door she'd imagined them naked against. Her fingers clenched around her keys and, instead, she imagined telling him she'd changed her mind and shutting it in his face.

She tried telling herself good looks and sex appeal were nothing. *Nothing.* They didn't influence Chloe Montgomery. Except Jordan was already on her doorstep, towering over her and making her swallow those lying, superficial and *treacherous* thoughts.

She realised she'd already partially closed the door on him. 'Sorry,' she murmured, motioning him in. 'My mind's everywhere tonight.'

'I imagine it is,' he said, stepping inside.

Up close, his sheer size in the cramped, dim foyer, lit only from the street lamp slanting through the glass door panels, accentuated their height difference. All her life she'd hated her lack of stature and accompanying feelings of insignificance. Yet somehow Jordan made her feel small and feminine and *not* insignificant in any way.

Not good if she was going to maintain her distance and keep things on a business level. She should have insisted on the safer option of conducting their conversation in its entirety at the restaurant. She'd been too quick to allow him to take control. 'Another coffee?' she asked, flicking on the passage light as she turned away and headed to the kitchen.

'Yes, please. Chloe, wait up.' A firm hand closed over her shoulder and he turned her to face him. 'You're not afraid of me, are you?' Both hands were on her shoulders now, his thumbs drawing tight little circles.

'Me? Afraid? Of you?' She choked out a half-laugh.

'Nervous as a kitten in a tiger's cage since we signed the paperwork.'

There was a lot more truth to that image than she wanted to think about. Jordan radiated that big-cat power and dominance—she could feel it tingling through his fingers and deep along her collarbones, turning them and every other extremity to rubber.

And so help her, Chloe Montgomery, who refused to allow others to dictate her life, who strenuously avoided the type of testosterone-fuelled, take-charge man that was Jordan, wanted to surrender to all that male dominance. Craved more of his lips on hers—and wherever else he wanted to put them—again.

She stiffened her spine and took a deliberate step away, only to end up with her back against the wall. Had she learned nothing in the past couple of years? 'It's myself I'm nervous of—if that makes sense.'

'Yeah. It does.' The massage stopped and he trailed his hands lightly over her shoulders, down her arms and up again, his eyes staring into hers with a smile that matched his mouth.

'You can't keep your thoughts off us getting naked together either.'

A distressed sound bubbled up her throat and fiery heat exploded into her cheeks. Was it that obvious?

'And how it's going to be when I come deep inside you,' he went on in a kind of murmur that swept up Chloe's spine like a big tabby cat's hot, wet tongue, making her shiver—in a dangerously delicious way. 'But that's not what we're about, not what we've agreed on, and it bothers you.'

'No, I… Yes…' This whole one-sided, erotic conversation *bothered* her.

And the fact that somehow, without her noticing, he'd moved closer so that the front of his shirt was brushing against her bodice while her useless arms hung limp. Only her fingers curled and uncurled at her sides.

He toyed with the tips of her hair as if he'd never seen fair hair before. 'Rest easy, Blondie, it'll be *you* inviting *me*,' he assured her, his deep voice resonating against her breasts and making her nipples tight and achy.

'*Me* inviting *you*.'

A slow confident smile spread across his features. 'You're worried about how that's going to work. Trust me, it'll work just fine.'

Trust me, Chloe.

'I am *not* worried because I intend to stay away from you as much as possible. And don't call me Blondie.'

'What will I call you, then? We should have pet names for each other, don't you think?'

'No. And there's that clause in the agreement that states—'

'We're not talking coercion here, *Blondie*,' he said smoothly. 'And we both know it.'

Drawing herself up taller, she dared to meet his blue-eyed intensity, but only succeeded in bumping up against another bit that she was sure hadn't been there a moment ago…and she froze, which was odd since she felt so, so hot. 'It's strictly business—you said so yourself.' Her words were crisp, cool and PA efficient to counteract the heat emanating between their bodies. 'You laid out the terms very clearly.'

'That's true.' Leaning down, he traced the neckline of her dress with a finger. 'Just because we have a business arrangement, doesn't mean it has to be all work. We can still keep it professional—' he removed his finger from the top of her dress and placed his palm flat on the wall beside her head '—but there's no reason we can't make it a bit of a holiday as well.'

She stared up at him, hair burnished teak by the suspended old-gold light in the foyer, not trusting herself to argue with his thought process. But a holiday fling? With one's business partner? *And* keep it professional? Wasn't going to happen.

She lifted her chin. 'You said our arrangement had nothing to do with the fact that you were attracted to me.'

'It doesn't.' He grinned, revealing even white teeth. 'We'll keep business and personal separate.'

'So what's this evening about, then? The *now* part of this evening.'

'Getting better acquainted.' His gaze slid to her lips. 'Isn't that what you said earlier?'

'I... Yes.' Didn't have to mean anything sexual, right? Of course they needed to get to know each other better. She could feel her legs giving way, her back sliding down the wall. 'But I don't think kissing's a good idea...'

'Why not? We really need to practise if we're to pull off the newlyweds charade.'

'No PDA's in Dubai, remember, so it's *really* not necessary. Since we won't be kissing in public. Or anywhere else...'

'But it'll give us that aura of implied intimacy. You know that look you see between two people that signals to the rest of the world that they're lovers?'

Her head bobbed once. 'Uh-huh…' Just as she recognised the look he was giving her now signalled *Danger: Intimacy Ahead*.

'Whisky eyes.' His breath feathered over her lips as he looked at her, his cobalt eyes dark with desire. 'I could get intoxicated just looking at them.'

'Seductive words.' And she refused to be seduced so easily. 'So were you intoxicated the last time you kissed me?'

'Stone-cold sober, as a matter of fact. And it was hardly a kiss.'

And she'd have agreed with him no matter how devastatingly intimate the kiss had seemed at the time, but before she could get a word out his mouth pounced on hers. Bold, predatory and without warning.

Reacting on instinct, her hands rushed up to push at his chest—to push him away—but her fingers had a mind of their own; they clutched at his jacket lapels and held on tight. Forget keeping her distance—how could she push him away when right now she wanted his mouth on hers more than air? Her eyes slid shut.

He deepened the kiss and she answered, her lips parting willingly beneath his demanding tongue. His taste was dark and rich, smooth and velvety—a moan rose up her throat— those *after-dinner delights* she'd been thinking of earlier and then some.

He dragged his hands down her sides, over her waist, the flare of her hips. Lower. Big hands spreading across her buttocks, tucking her in close, so that she could feel the hot, hard length of him.

Heat and sizzle and danger. It was like being swept up in a forest fire and her entire body was turning to flame. She might have tried again to stop him and to make some sense of…whatever this was, but her brain was frazzled from all the heat and the message wasn't getting through to her limbs.

He lifted his lips a fraction. 'Now *that's* a kiss,' he murmured. She felt his hands lift away from her body, coolness drifting in to take their place. She pried her heavy-lidded eyes open to see him staring down at her, a gleam in his gaze that had nothing to do with the hall light's reflection.

Ah... 'Mmm-hmm.' She cleared the sigh from her throat and admitted, 'That's a kiss all right...' Pressing her tingling lips together, she kept her back propped against the wall, still captive beneath his gaze. 'I just need to...' *breathe*. 'I need time. To think.' If she still had any brain cells left intact, that was.

'Think fast, then. We're booked on the evening flight out tomorrow night. It's non-stop, which gives us roughly forty hours before we arrive in Dubai.'

'What?' She felt some of her precious independence trickle away. 'You booked before I agreed,' she shot at him.

'I was—'

'Confident,' she snapped. 'Yes, I get that.'

He nodded, his eyes smiling. 'It pays to think positive.'

She glared. 'You even asked if I had prior commitments. You had no intention of letting me honour them, did you?'

No response. Conversation over. His body heat mingled with musky male scent and suddenly he was too close, the space between them too confining, and she shuffled to one side.

He remained still, allowing her to step away. But she knew tigers were motionless just before they moved in for the kill. She tore her eyes free and moved as swiftly as her rubber legs allowed towards the kitchen.

She heard Jordan's heavy footsteps on the floorboards. His dark flavour lingered on her lips, her tongue. 'Coffee,' she muttered, then over her shoulder, 'We don't have a coffee machine. It's instant or nothing.'

'Instant's fine,' he said, all easy-to-please, but she could feel his eyes on her back and something potent and irresist-ible shivered down her spine. That big tabby cat tongue again.

She slowed at the doorway to the lounge room and ges-tured inside without looking at him. 'Why don't you make yourself comfortable in there? Put the heater on if you want. I won't be long.'

Jordan sank onto the couch but he was hardly comfortable. With the way his body reacted to this woman, he wondered if he'd ever be comfortable again. A way too full-on, over-the-top response for a girl who wasn't supposed to be his type.

The last thing he needed was a gas wall furnace; what he needed was a cold shower. He tried focusing on his sur-roundings. A couple of mismatched armchairs, coffee table covered in a Christmas print cloth and topped with an un-tidy pile of magazines. Travellers' photos on the walls; pre-sumably her house-mates', the flight attendants. Nothing in the room said Chloe. Maybe she'd not had time to put her mark on the place or maybe she never stopped long enough to make a place home.

Despite her insistence that she loved her solo lifestyle, he found the thought of her alone and itinerant for so long a lit-tle sad. Her words and actions proved she also believed fam-ily was important despite how they'd treated her. He found that sad as well.

'Couldn't remember if you take sugar.'

He turned at the sound of her voice. 'I gave it up.'

'Good for you.' She handed him a cup, then moved to the gas heater mounted on the wall. 'You're not cold?'

'No, but go ahead if you are. Or you could come over here.' He patted the empty space beside him.

'I think we both know that's not a good idea.' Her eyes swirled with more of that heated awareness but beneath it he saw a reserve, a barrier, that hadn't been there before he'd kissed her against that wall. She stood in front of the grille, hugging her mug to her lips while the heater powered up. 'When I mentioned "getting acquainted", I meant everyday things we should know about each other like…'

'Family,' he said for her. 'You can start.'

'Okay,' she said slowly. 'I have a brother and a sister, both much older than me. Donna's married to Jason, an accountant, and they have a teenage son. She has a degree in arts and another in classical studies but she's been a stay-at-home mum for the past fifteen years. Caleb's a physio with a degree in architecture on the side and married to Jenny, his receptionist, who's studying natural medicine.'

Wow. Academic over-achievers, all of them. No wonder Chloe felt she didn't fit in. He frowned as something occurred to him. 'Donna's the one expecting your financial rescue package?'

Chloe sipped her coffee, then nodded. 'She's the one who kept in contact, as infrequent as that is.'

'So tell me something,' he said, slowly. 'With two older siblings, why is the onus on you to bail the parents out?'

'Caleb's mother-in-law's a widow, she's terminally ill and he's footing the medical bills. Brother-in-law, Jason, the accountant who should know better, lost his money in a failed business venture last year. Donna's "looking for suitable work".' She shrugged. 'Donna's been "looking for suitable work" for the past ten of those fifteen years.' She raised her mug towards him. 'Your turn.'

'You know about Dad. My mother's not in my life and I'm an only child.'

She studied him over the rim of her mug. 'You're going to need to do better than that.'

The old bad lodged in his gut, the familiar lead ball he'd carried around since childhood. He didn't want to talk about the woman who'd given birth to him. Ina was nothing to him.

She didn't exist. But he couldn't ignore the fact that she was married to the man who wanted this deal as much as Jordan.

His emotions must have showed because her eyes turned soft and compassionate. 'I'm sorry, Jordan, if it's a painful topic for you, but I need to know more if we're going to do this thing. Is she…?'

She trailed off awkwardly and Jordan helped her out. 'Ina's alive and doing very nicely for herself.' Jaw tight, he filled Chloe in on his mother's second marriage with the owner of his business rival. He did *not* delve further into their relationship and was relieved when Chloe didn't push it.

'I'm understanding more about why this is all so important to you,' she said, still watching him with those liquid sympathy eyes. 'I'm sorry you and your mum can't get on.'

He'd never seen that look directed at him before. Or maybe he'd never looked for it. He wasn't looking for it now; it was just…there. Was he seeing more in Chloe's eyes than he saw in other women's? Which begged the question, why? He wasn't sure he wanted to know.

He did know that he didn't want sympathy, didn't want what it stirred up inside him, or the associated feelings that came with it. 'I like to win.'

It wasn't revenge or even satisfaction he was seeking. This deal with Dubai was about honouring his father and closure.

Chloe nodded. 'And I like to finish what I start.'

As long as it doesn't take too long, he finished for her. Frankly, the fact that she liked to finish things surprised him.

So, this little adventure wouldn't take long and the reward was huge, for both of them. He pushed up from the couch and raised his mug in salute. 'We *will* win this, Chloe.'

She raised her mug too, and smiled, her eyes alive with enthusiasm. 'Dubai, here we come.'

CHAPTER SIX

'How NEWLYWED ARE we talking?' Chloe asked when they got down to business ten minutes later. She'd unearthed a note-pad from the kitchen and was committing their ideas to paper for future reference. She'd drawn up two columns: one for plans—flights, accommodation, sightseeing she intended to get in while she was there; the other for 'getting acquainted'. Such as background and personal details, real and invented. It kept her hands busy, her eyes down and also helped her to keep everything on a professional level.

'We're combining business with our honeymoon.'

A small smile hooked the corner of her mouth. 'That doesn't make you a very good husband.'

'But you're a very supportive wife and you understand my commitment to business. Besides, once you'd manipulated me into popping the question, you didn't want to wait another day.'

Manipulated? She did look up at him then and noticed a tightening around his mouth, which transformed into a lop-sided grin when he caught her staring at him.

'But I'm happy you did, Blondie,' he assured her quickly.

'Yeah? For how long?' She couldn't imagine anyone ma-nipulating Jordan but the stormy depths of his gaze told her someone had tried.

'Eternity. Right?'

She narrowed her eyes. 'Have you been married before?'

'No.'

Do I look stupid? She received his message loud and clear. His blatant cynicism annoyed her. 'You'd better change that attitude before we get there or it'll be game over before we start,' she said, frowning back at her notes. 'Seriously.'

'I am serious. How can you doubt it after the time and effort and expense I'm putting in to make it happen?'

'Right.' She wrote COMMITMENT PHOBIC in her 'getting acquainted' column. She believed in marriage when two people loved and trusted each other and were committed to making it work. But after Stewart, she didn't believe that she personally could do the trust or even the long-term bit. Or maybe she was afraid to believe.

Did that make her as commitment phobic as him? she wondered momentarily. Not at all, she told herself. She wasn't phobic, just…careful. Right?

'I'm also serious about sharing a little pleasure around the business aspect,' he said.

'Well, maybe I'm not.' She added APPROACH AT OWN PERIL to the list and slapped her notepad shut.

'You were enjoying it fine a few moments ago.' His eyes dared her to take issue with the inconvenient truth.

'You didn't give me time to…to change my mind,' she said, dismissing their kiss. 'I wasn't ready.'

'You've been ready since the last time we bumped lips.' Bracing his forearms on his knees, he gave her that sexy grin that made her want to throw herself onto the couch next to him and beg him to do it again.

'No.'

'Come on, you were curious. And it was good, right?'

She exhaled through her nostrils. 'Okay. Fine. It was good.'

'As good as you expected?'

He just had to keep pushing, didn't he? 'It was right up

there with white-water rafting, New Year's Eve sky shows and soft-centre chocolates. Satisfied?'

'Not nearly.'

'But it's not going to happen again,' she went on, tapping her notebook with her pen. 'It muddies our business relationship.'

His grin widened. 'I disagree. Our business relationship is about making our "recent marriage" look legitimate to our target audience.'

'We can still do that. *I* can still do that. It's what you're paying me for.' Which reminded her—the purpose of tonight's meeting. 'Think of me as a conservative, no-nonsense, PA…'

'Hard to imagine when none of those labels suit you.'

'Then *don't* think or imagine, just listen and discuss.' Flipping open her notepad again, she clicked her pen. 'Accommodation—'

'Already taken care of.' He grinned, the lines around his eyes crinkling. He shrugged when she glared. 'Can't help it—I do like an enthusiastic partner.'

An image played behind her eyes. A very active, very inappropriate image. *He means business partner, Chloe.* Didn't he? 'I… You're making this difficult.'

'Tell you what, we can go over this tomorrow evening at the airport or onboard our flight,' he said, setting his mug on the coffee table in front of him. 'It's late. We'll call it a night.'

She let out a sigh. 'You don't know how relieved I am to hear that. I have so much to organise. To pack.'

But her entire wardrobe fitted into one large suitcase and her relief was short-lived. The Jordan Blackstone she'd seen online dated stunning, statuesque women who knew how to dress to impress. He'd have been better off choosing someone with a sense of fashion who already knew the role to play the part. 'I'm not a fashionista—I'm more of a jeans and T-shirt kind of girl. What am I expected to wear?'

'We'll have a day to shop when we get there.' He rose, pulling a bunch of keys from his trouser pocket and drawing her attention to where it shouldn't be drawn. 'I'll call you in the morning.'

She followed his broad shape down the hall, trying not to admire the back of his tanned neck below the neat trim of dark hair. That earlier anticipation was sparking again, like two live wires touching.

Was he going to try to kiss her good night?

Was she going to let him?

But he opened the door then leaned close, kissed her chastely on the cheek. ''Night, Blondie.' He stepped out into the evening.

''Night…' She felt like a teenager, giddy with first-date fever, hanging on to the doorframe and wishing he'd come back and kiss her again, properly this time. 'And thanks for the wonderful dinner.'

His playful gaze didn't waver but a hint of something more intimate infused the cerulean with shades of midnight, making her heart leap beneath her breastbone.

'The first of many wonderful things,' he said, jingling his keys in his hand. 'Now get some sleep.'

She intended to. She had a feeling she was going to need it. *The first of many wonderful things.* His words—a promise?—danced in her head like sugar plum fairies. It was going to be next to impossible to keep her mind focused where it needed to be.

It was going to be next to impossible to keep his mind focused where it needed to be. Jordan lowered his window and let the winter's damp chill wrap around his neck as he drove back to his apartment. Perhaps it would help cool his blood and redirect it to his brain instead of his groin.

For God's sake.

He barely noticed that the view of Melbourne's CBD through his windscreen was blurred with rain—he was too preoccupied with thinking about the way Chloe's hair had felt against his fingers. Its cool, delicate fragrance and how it would feel brushing low over his belly as she—

Damn. He blew out a disgusted breath, shifting in his seat and tightening his grip on the wheel. He'd never had trouble focusing and he wasn't starting now. Chloe Montgomery might be his current red-hot fantasy but she was a means to an end and he was forgetting what was important here. She was being paid to play a role, and with her help he was finally going to settle an old debt.

But he recalled her stunned surprise when he'd planted that first proper kiss on her soft lips and couldn't help the smile that touched his mouth. The delightful way she'd tried to push away only to change her mind. The feel of her firm breasts against his chest. Her taste—sweet and spice and everything nice.

He turned into his apartment complex's underground parking. The security door rose with a hum. Not the only thing humming, he thought, still smiling, as he drove through then manoeuvred into his parking spot. He couldn't wait for tomorrow evening. To see her again. To be on his way. To move forward with the next stage of his life.

Yeah, everything about this trip was going to be sweet.

Dawn was grey with a dusky pink glow, the city's twinkling blanket of lights spread out below when Jordan embarked on a rigorous morning workout a few sleepless hours later.

In the interim, he'd spoken at length with Qasim and everything was arranged with their meeting in two days' time.

He'd confirmed the accommodation, the best that money could buy, and organised a driver to be on call while they were there.

He was cycling hard and going nowhere to the beat of his favourite rock band when a lemon sun, partially obscured by high-rises, lifted into the sky at seven-thirty. Through his gym's floor-to-ceiling glass, Jordan watched the caterpillars of traffic below crawl along and figured Chloe should be up by now.

Still pedalling, he disconnected his music, scrolled to her number and turned his phone on loudspeaker.

She answered on the second ring—''Lo'—filling the room with her husky, sleepy, too-close-for-comfort murmur.

'You're not still in bed, are you?'

A pause, followed by a shushing, shifting, tantalisingly erotic sound that seemed to reach through the speaker to stroke his crotch. 'Why?'

Why? Because he didn't want her to be still in bed *because* he didn't want to imagine her still warm and soft with sleep, firm flat tummy exposed beneath rumpled flannelette pyjamas. He stepped up his pace on the bike and said, 'I took you for an early riser.'

'Did you? Why?'

Hell if he knew. 'So you're not?'

'Not what?' Breathless pause. 'In bed?'

'No—an early riser.' He blew out a harried breath. 'Are you still in bed or not?'

'No. Actually I've just stepped out of the shower.'

Naked. Worse, much worse. She was naked, and the shifting sound was more like a rubbing sound now that he knew it had to be a towel. Against heat-pinkened flesh. He let out a long, low groan.

'Are you okay?' she said sharply. 'What are you doing?'

'You shouldn't ask a man that question first thing in the

morning when you're naked and rubbing yourself with a towel.'

He heard a slight catch of breath then, 'Oh… *Oh.*'

'I'm riding a bike, Chloe.' And damn uncomfortable it was, too.

'Where?'

'Home gym. I'd invite you over for breakfast,' he said, dismounting and heading to his en-suite, 'but the traffic's chaos.'

'I've eaten already.'

So she was a step ahead of him. 'Flannelette pyjamas,' he murmured, toeing off his trainers along the way.

'What?'

'Never mind.' He turned his attention to more immediate matters as he stripped down and flung his jocks in the laundry basket. 'We need to shop this morning. I'll drop by around twelve. Be packed, we won't be going home after.'

'I thought we were going shopping in Dubai?'

'There's something we need to get before we leave.'

'Twelve's okay…but—'

'I'll see you then,' he told her before she could quiz him further, and disconnected.

He padded back to his bedroom for a change of clothes. He had two more calls to make. 'Hey,' he replied when Sadiq answered. 'Hope I'm not catching you at an inconvenient time?'

'On my way out but I was going to call you later this morning anyway since I hadn't heard from you. What's happening with Dubai?'

'Yeah. I've talked with Qasim again. The meeting's all set and I'll be flying out later this evening.'

'Sounds promising.'

Jordan pulled a caramel toffee-coloured jumper from a drawer. 'I'm taking Chloe with me.'

'Chloe.' Jordan could almost hear Sadiq's ears prick up.

'I took your advice.'

'So you're stealing her away from Dana?' Sadiq chuckled. 'Dana won't be pleased—Chloe's her new favourite worker.'

'I'll write dear Dana a cheque to cover a fill-in temp's wages for a couple of weeks—she'll be pleased enough.'

'How did you manage it?' Sadiq queried. 'Chloe didn't look too happy to see you at Sunday brunch. Did you work the Blackstone charm again?'

Jordan rifled through his sock drawer for his favourites, tossing a couple of orphans on the floor in the process. 'I simply made her an offer she couldn't refuse.'

'And…'

'Let's just say we have an arrangement.'

'Sounds…cosy.'

'A business arrangement. And not for public knowledge.' Not even Sadiq need know the details, except Jordan had the feeling the man had it figured out already. 'Not a word to anyone, my trusted friend,' he cautioned as he headed for the shower. 'I want the press kept well out of it.' He paused. 'And if Qasim and you talk at any stage and I happen to come up in conversation…just play along with whatever he says, okay?'

'Aah.'

Perceptive man, Sadiq. 'Thanks. Gotta go.'

'Good luck.'

Chloe was out on the veranda with her travel-battered bag by eleven forty-five. She'd left a note for her absent house-mates on the kitchen table along with the next rent payment in cash. With her new-look bank balance that she was still getting used to, it had been easy peasy.

She'd also deposited a five-figure amount in her parents' account and it had only made a small dent in the overall balance. The knowledge blew her away. And there was still the other half of the payment expected at the end.

An icy wind snuck in under the roof and around the veranda posts, chilling her face, but she rubbed sweaty palms down her jeans. This trip was a whole new experience, like a scary fun park ride in a new dimension.

Dana had rung a couple of hours ago to wish her a successful trip. Chloe had detected a knowing smile in her boss's voice when she'd told her to 'take care and enjoy yourself'.

What had Jordan said to the woman? Or had Dana just assumed Chloe would be bowled over by his charm and ready to run off with him at the drop of a hat? She told herself as long as her job was still available when she came back, she didn't care what Dana assumed.

She was checking her watch for the zillionth time when a luxury car pulled up. Jordan unfolded his long body from the front passenger seat and stepped out to open the rear door. Dark glasses shielded his eyes. His caramel V-neck jumper over an open brown shirt and well-worn jeans that clung to his butt like a denim glove elicited a soft sigh of feminine appreciation from Chloe as she walked down the short path to the gate.

'Morning.' He smiled—a tempting smile that reminded her all over again of last night's kiss—and raised a hand in greeting. The wind tossed his hair so that it stood up in short tufts on top of his head.

'Morning.' She'd not seen him in casual clothes before. He almost looked like a different man—more accessible, more fun perhaps, than the corporate suited guy she was still getting acquainted with—but no less impressive. Or gorgeous, or sexy. Or beddable.

Bad thought, very bad thought. She mentally berated herself and whisked her trolley bag to the kerb. There was going to be none of that. She exchanged greetings with the uniformed driver as he loaded her bag into the boot.

'Right on time.' Jordan gestured her into the car.

'You sound surprised,' she said, climbing in.

'More like pleased.' He shut the door, rounded the boot, and climbed in beside her on the other side. Even though the car was more like a limo, his long legs took up most of the floor space, leaving her to cram up alongside. Or maybe he'd just engineered it that way.

'You make it sound as if men are the only ones capable of time management.'

'I've yet to meet a date who hasn't kept me waiting.'

With the high-maintenance, salon-treatment-three-times-a-week siliconed and Botoxed beauties she'd seen hanging on his arm in the glossy magazines, she didn't doubt it.

Or was she being unkind? Worse, jealous?

No, of course she wasn't. And because she was a big believer in punctuality being all about respect, she couldn't resist saying, 'You've been dating the wrong women, then.'

He was checking inside the pocket of his jacket that lay on the seat between them but his gaze shifted and focused on her. Not smiling. Prickles of heat rose up her neck, into her cheeks. He seemed to take an eternity before he said slowly, 'Maybe I have.'

Oh, no, she *had* sounded jealous. She wished she knew how he felt about that but she couldn't read his eyes behind his dark glasses. And she so wished she'd never spoken those petty little words just because those glossy glams got to her. Who was Chloe to tell Jordan Blackstone, millionaire, what kind of woman he needed?

Rather than try to explain her way out, she crossed her arms over her chest and glared out of the window as they neared the city. A tram rattled past as they drove along Collins Street, congested with lunch-time office workers. 'In case you've forgotten, this is not a date.'

'I haven't forgotten. It's much more important than that. Chloe, look at me.'

She continued to stare at the street-scape but his powerful

gaze on the back of her head drew her against her will—how did he continually manage that?

'Are you still okay with everything?' he asked. 'Because being defensive and prickly around me isn't going to help us.'

'I'm not being prickly…am I?' She deliberately breathed out, smoothed and relaxed taut muscles. 'I don't mean to be.'

'Just be aware of it when we're with other people,' he said as the car pulled into the kerb in front of a shiny black granite office building. 'Here we are.'

'Where, exactly?'

'We have an appointment.' Jordan withdrew his wallet from his jacket, slipped it into the back pocket of his jeans. 'You might want to put on your sunglasses,' he said, opening his door. 'I promised to protect you from the press but they're always where you least expect.'

She fished around in her bag while he came around the car to her side, then slid them on her face.

He hustled her towards the revolving glass door. 'What about our driver?' she asked as they approached the bank of elevators. 'I assume you know him?'

They stepped into an empty lift and he pressed the button for the tenth floor. 'He's a member of my staff here. I pay him to be discreet.'

She took off the glasses, put them in her bag. 'What do you mean by "here"?'

'Rivergold's head office is in Perth. I divide my time between the two cities.'

The doors slid open and they stepped out into a foyer with deep violet walls and concealed lighting. The word *Gilded* hovered above the reception desk in flowing gold script.

Jewellery, Chloe realised. Expensive, exclusive jewellery. She discovered first up that Jordan and the receptionist—Trudi—were on a first-name basis.

Trudi was all smiles for Jordan—naturally—and led them

down a wide corridor, keyed a code into a heavy door and showed them into a comfortable room overlooking the city. She offered them refreshments, Jordan ordered water for the both of them, then another staff member called Trudi away, which left the two of them alone.

Chloe had always insisted jewellery didn't match her lifestyle. She'd choose an airline ticket to an exotic destination over pretty but essentially useless baubles any day. 'I…um. I'm not much of a jewellery person.'

He glanced at her hands. 'I've noticed. But we need wedding rings.'

'Wedding rings…' she echoed. *Of course, wedding rings.*

'You're okay with that, I hope.'

'I just hadn't given it a thought. But this place is…' *ridiculously expensive and overpriced.* She waved her hand to encompass the leather armchairs, the glass-topped table for private showings with its neatly rolled up little black velvet mat on one end. 'We could've gone somewhere cheaper, is all I'm saying. After all, it's not as if it's for real.'

But for a brief heartbeat in time, she wondered how it would feel if it were and something inside her yearned before she shoved it away, deep in that place where she'd never find it again. Never wanted to find it again. Not with a man like Jordan—rich, powerful, gorgeous. Like Stewart.

A heartbreak waiting to happen.

She realised he was staring her down, his eyes a shade of cool logic. 'I own a *gold* mine, we're meeting a *gold* manufacturer in the hope that he and I will do business. With *gold.* What if he or his wife asks to look at your shiny new ring? And even if they don't ask, do you think he's not going to notice?'

'Oh…of course.' She closed her eyes briefly, embarrassed at her own stupidity. 'I hadn't thought about it.' And she needed to start—thinking about it. All of it. Like how *not* in his class she was and how impossible anything long-term or meaningful between them could ever be.

A smartly dressed middle-aged man entered the room with half a dozen jewellery trays. 'Jordan. So good to see you.' He beamed as he set the trays on the glass table and shook hands with Jordan, then extended his hand to Chloe. 'And Miss Montgomery, welcome.'

'Chloe, this is Kieron,' Jordan said as she shook the man's hand.

'Thank you, and call me Chloe.'

'This must be an exciting time for you.' He smiled, clearly expecting an answer.

'Yeah…um…' How much did he know? She glanced at Jordan for help but he was checking out the goodie trays. Damn him. 'We're…um…looking forward to it…' Whatever *it* was.

'What's your colour preference in gold?' Jordan asked without turning around.

She shifted, vaguely awkward in Kieron's presence and cursing Jordan some more for not paying attention. 'I'm not particular.'

'In that case we'll go with yellow,' he said. 'Sit down and let's get started.'

Kieron spread out the mat and placed a tray on the table, exquisite rings, all embedded with diamonds and other precious stones and sparkling in the down lights.

Jordan selected a couple of highly visual and elaborate rings and set them on the mat. 'Which do you prefer?'

'Do you have a plain gold band?' she almost pleaded with him. 'Thin. Plain.'

Jordan met her eyes. 'Kieron, can you give us a few moments, please?'

'Of course. I'll see what I can find in plain gold—'

'No need,' Jordan said, his gaze not leaving hers. 'I'm

sure we'll find something here. I'll give you a call when we're done.'

'What do you mean?' she demanded in a tight, low voice almost before the man had closed the door behind him. 'I don't want—'

'It's not about what you want. You—rather, *we*—need something ostentatious.'

'What about you? Your ring? Is this marriage going to be one based on inequality?'

He opened his palm, revealing a thick gold ring. 'Men's wedding band channel-set with black diamonds.' He set it in front of her. 'I can't have mine outshining yours.'

'Why can't *you* choose something simpler?'

'Because the ring has to make a statement. It has to shout, "We're married and exclusive and we want the world to know". It also says only Rivergold's gold is good enough for the love of my life.'

'So Gilded is your business?'

'One of them. What about this?' He picked up a smaller ring from the tray, a band of gold filigree, its dainty vine-leaf pattern studded with tiny diamonds. Kind of classic yet modern and delicate.

She told herself it wasn't the most gorgeous ring she'd ever seen. It wouldn't fit. It wasn't practical. But this time perhaps she could have the exotic destination *and* the pretty bauble. And oh… She sighed at the misty-eyed romance of it.

And just for once, she *wanted* misty-eyed romantic and impractical. It wasn't forever, she reassured herself. It didn't mean she was going to fall into bed with him—or worse, into love. No way. No how. No—

'I think it'll suit you. Try it.' Jordan reached across the table and took her hand.

As if from a distance, she watched him slide the ring onto her finger. The abrading sensation of his fingertips against

hers, every nerve ending he touched tingling like tiny pin-
pricks of fire. Her hand looked so small in his. His fingers
were long and tanned, his wrist thick and dusted with dark
hair.

She couldn't seem to move, couldn't seem to drag her eyes
away from their linked hands. It was like being in someone
else's dream—someone else's because Chloe no longer allowed herself to dream such fantasies.

He eased the ring over her knuckle. Perfect fit. Perfect
design. Perfect.

'Chloe...' he said, deep and dreamy and masculine. *Will
you be my wife?*

CHAPTER SEVEN

HEART SONG FOR the romantic soul.

Chloe might have sighed or murmured, but the touch of Jordan's finger beneath her chin as he tilted her face up to him shattered her dreamy illusions as loudly and irrevocably as fine glass smashing on marble.

'The ring,' she heard him say over the echoes still reverberating in her mind. The *only* thing he'd said.

She stared up at him, caught in the blue depths of his gaze. 'Yes?'

'What do you think?'

I think I'm starting to imagine stuff. 'About the ring?'

A perplexed expression crossed his face. 'Yes, the ring— what else?'

'Right. The ring...' *Of course, what else?* She breathed in deep, ordering herself to focus, adjusting to the sight of it glittering on her hand. 'It's lovely.' Oh, she could so spin a softly romantic story out of this—

'Good. Let's go, then.'

His emotionless tone brought her back to reality with a thud. She rubbed the fingers of her right hand over her left knuckles, then flexed them. 'Shall I leave it on?'

He nodded once. 'Wouldn't do to lose it now, would it?'

She noticed he was already wearing his when he pressed a buzzer on the table and she felt a flutter around her heart.

Even though it was for show purposes only, that no words had been exchanged—not even a meaningful glance—the symbolism gave her the odd feeling that they were connected somehow. That they belonged together.

Of course, that was dumb and stupid and very, very dangerous. She'd return the ring when they were done and that would be the end of it.

Still, she needed a moment to get over herself, so when Kieron met them at the door Chloe did a quick trip to the restrooms while the two men continued to Reception.

As she washed her hands she checked that the precious band wasn't too loose on her finger. Where had his ring appeared from? she wondered. She'd seen no men's rings on the tray. But everything was happening so fast, she could forgive herself for getting confused.

When she returned, they were deep in conversation. 'If it wasn't for you, I don't know where we'd be,' she heard Kieron say.

'Okay, all set,' she said, to announce her presence in case she heard something she wasn't supposed to.

Jordan clasped the other man's shoulder. 'Look after that special lady of yours.'

Kieron clasped him back and Chloe wondered what Jordan had done for his employee and his special lady that inspired such awe and gratitude.

She decided to ask him about it as his driver chauffeured them to a restaurant for lunch.

'Kieron worked for us in Perth. His wife's chronically ill and the specialised treatment she needs is only available in Melbourne, so we transferred him.'

His manner was casual, almost dismissive, but Chloe had seen the admiration on the man's face and sensed there was more to it than a simple location transfer. 'And...?' she prompted.

'And what?'

'Tell me more. What else does Jordan Blackstone do for his staff?'

He looked away, out of the window. 'The man had no private health insurance; they were renting basic accommodation. I'm his employer—I do what I can.'

A warm feeling spread across her chest. 'Good for you. You're a compassionate boss. More than that, you're a generous one.'

'I can afford to be.' He sounded curt and irritated. 'Don't make a big deal of it.'

'Okay.' She smiled at him and reached out to touch his arm. 'I won't mention that you're a generous boss again.'

She could have sworn he flinched at her touch. 'Just so we're clear,' he said, still watching the traffic. 'I'm not *your* boss—we're equals. Partners.'

'*Business* partners,' she finished, in case he had the wrong idea. It was nothing more. Right?

In a private dining room with a view of the Docklands and Westgate Bridge, they discussed the finer details of the trip, covering etiquette, customs and dress code. They were keeping their story simple and as close to the truth as possible. They'd met in Melbourne a couple of months ago and it had been love at first sight.

Jordan explained that after the formal introductions, Chloe wouldn't be expected to participate in any business discussions. Any strong feminist ideals she might have were to be left at Tullamarine Airport. She would be entertained by the sheikh's wife and the women in his family. There would be an evening dinner or two but during the day she'd be free to do as she chose. A driver had already been arranged to take her wherever she wanted to go.

By mutual agreement, they filled in some of their time at

the airport separately so as not to attract any unwanted media attention. Chloe wandered the duty-free shops for a couple of hours then returned to the relative privacy of the business lounge and read a couple of women's magazines while Jordan studied some heavy-looking manual he'd brought with him and surfed the net on his laptop.

And every so often she'd feel the ring's unfamiliar weight on her finger or catch its prettiness winking in the light. Then her eyes would flick to Jordan's hand and she'd see his wide band and a strange feeling like silken ribbons would flutter through her, twining around her heart, making her restless and cheated somehow. Dissatisfied.

Over a late light meal served on board the flight, they relaxed and enjoyed a movie together, although at times Chloe sensed Jordan's tension. Whether it was business related, she didn't know, but he didn't seem inclined to pursue anything romantic and that was a huge relief. Really. She was *not* disappointed.

This trip wasn't the travel experience she was accustomed to. The aircraft's business-class luxury gave them privacy in their individual wraparound fully reclining seats, and at midnight Chloe donned her eyeshades to try to get at least a couple of hours' sleep.

It didn't help. Excitement buzzed through her limbs so that in the end she tossed away the eyeshades and let her flickering personal TV screen lull her rioting thoughts. She couldn't wait till morning when she'd step into a different world and a different life.

She just needed to remember that the life part and the *wife* part weren't for real. It was short and it was temporary.

The glint of gold caught his eye as Jordan turned the page of the document on the aircraft's table in front of him. He stared at the sight of the familiar ring on his finger. How long had it been since that day he and Lynette Dixon had decided they were getting married?

Six years.

And in the madness of that moment they'd walked into a local jewellery shop along the coast and bought their wedding rings—a man who owned his own gold-mining company, for God's sake. He still didn't know how she'd managed it. How she'd manipulated him into it. The way his mother had manipulated and deceived his father his entire life.

He turned to the night-dark window where the aircraft's flashing red light swept rhythmically over the engine, but it was Lynette's picture-perfect face he saw reflected there.

He'd met the blonde bombshell at uni and fallen for her with the speed—and devastation—of an avalanche down a ski-slope. Jordan Blackstone, who could charm any girl he set his sights on with a virtual crook of his little finger, had become the charmed. At twenty-six, when he'd been old enough and wise enough to know better, he'd lost his brains, his willpower, his self-respect. And his heart.

Because on the morning they'd arranged to elope to Las Vegas, he'd learned he'd been played for the fool he was.

He twisted the ring that suddenly felt thick and heavy and confining. Yes, he should have known better. Hadn't he lived through a prime example of what not to do? He'd seen the power his mother had wielded over his father, and all because Fraser Blackstone had loved Ina without reservation. All his life Fraser had been a slave to that love. Blind to his wife's treachery—or he'd chosen to ignore it. Either way, it just went to prove that love made you weak.

Which was why he'd kept the ring. A reminder of his foolishness. A reminder that, without due care, women could be a costly distraction. A reminder of his vow never to allow it to happen again.

He would be no woman's slave. His will would prevail.

When he wanted a woman to share his bed, *he* would do the choosing, not the other way round. And that woman might touch his body—in any way she pleased—but no woman would touch his heart.

At sunrise the aircraft touched down in Dubai. The desert air was dry and cool after the plane's stale air conditioning as they walked out of the terminal.

Chloe breathed deeply. Aside from the odour of aviation fuel, everything smelled foreign and exciting.

'Ready to go, Mrs Blackstone?' Jordan said beside her.

'Ready, Mr Blackstone.'

A uniformed driver was waiting to take them to the city and opened the limo door. *'Ahlan wa Sahlan.'* Welcome.

'Ahlan bik.' Jordan waited while Chloe settled herself, then slid in beside her. 'Get ready to be amazed,' he said.

'Okay.' He sounded little-boy excited and she glanced at him, saw the enthusiasm reflected in his eyes. 'Are we talking about something in particular?'

He smiled but didn't enlighten her. 'Wait and see.'

So she immersed herself in the scenery, from the low sand dunes that came up to the edge of the road in some places to the sky's palette of pink and tangerine against unique silver-glinting architecture spiralling into the stratosphere. They travelled over the Dubai Creek, and everywhere she looked construction was frenetic. Cranes, roadworks and traffic hazards, dust.

Dubai's famous seven-star hotel suddenly reared up in front of them, its proud billowing shape catching the sun. 'Now that's something amazing. Is this what you meant…?' She trailed off as the vehicle turned onto the dedicated road that led to the grand entrance. 'Are we staying here? *Here? Really?*'

Bubbles of excitement fizzed through her veins. She

shifted to fling her arms around him, reining herself back just in time. She needed to maintain a respectful distance while she was here. Not only because this was the United Arab Emirates but because right now she wasn't sure she'd be able to stop if she started.

But he didn't seem bothered about the etiquette they'd discussed the other night. They were in a private car with tinted windows, after all. Leaning close so that his lips touched her hair, he murmured against her ear. 'A honeymoon to remember, Blondie.'

She told herself flirting was okay. Harmless. 'I'm sure it will be. *Pookie.*'

His brows shot up, his lips forming the word, but no sound came out. She meant the whole Arabian experience, not what he was obviously thinking she meant with that name—sex on tap—but she smiled and patted his arm, feeling safe in the knowledge he'd not touch her unless she allowed it.

Moments later as they entered through the massive revolving door her breath eased out in awe. The outside view of golden sand curving around the ultramarine to turquoise sea was echoed in the atrium that seemed to rise forever.

A row of staff greeted them as if they were royalty, offering miniature steaming towels, dishes of dates, coffee poured from exotic-shaped carafes.

It was all about the bling—in the mirrored walls, the ceilings, the rich crimson drapes, the waterfall over blocks of green and gold tumbling down beside an escalator. They were still sipping from tiny coffee cups as they shot skywards in a glass-walled elevator.

Their split-level suite had breathtaking views of the beach framed by the building's white bars and steel rope. While staff delivered their luggage and immediately unpacked their belongings, Jordan took charge of a master remote that controlled everything from curtains to TV and music to opening the door and calling up room service.

Chloe explored. A swimming-pool-sized spa set in polished granite, gold fittings, a gallery of mirrors and a view of the skyline. An opulent office with every amenity at one's fingertips. Bowls of tropical flowers on polished tables.

By the time she found the bedroom, their luggage had been unpacked, their cases removed out of sight. The vast purple-hued Arabian nights fantasy bed with its gold trimmed canopy dominated the room, reminding her of a flying carpet.

But there was only one.

And there were two of *them*… Images of soaring into the night sky filled her head…and those images didn't involve aircraft. She turned away. *Remember why you can't. Remember why you're here.*

She didn't want to jeopardise this important deal that meant so much to Jordan because of something she'd done or not done. She was being paid a sheikh's ransom to support him. Her feelings for him weren't professional, never had been, so it was already a struggle to stick to the business relationship she herself had insisted on.

She found him sitting in a bright alcove overlooking the sea and slicing a mango onto a gold-rimmed plate. She sat down opposite him and looked at the opulence about her. 'I could get seriously used to this.'

'Enjoy, but don't get used to it,' he suggested. 'It's a one-off.'

'Ah, yes, the honeymoon. And you're writing it off as a business expense, right?' She smiled. 'As your bride, I'm still annoyed about that.'

He offered her the plate. 'But you couldn't wait to be married, remember?' He raised a brow. 'Which reminds me— *Pookie?*'

'It was your idea to have pet names.' She took a slice of

the fruit, slipped it between her lips and savoured its cool, pungent taste on her tongue.

'There's a certain eroticism attached to that particular endearment, however, and it *does* conjure images.' Hot cerulean eyes lapped at her.

'It does?' It did. She felt the mango sliding down the wrong way and cleared her throat, which suddenly felt tight and scratchy.

'Maybe you've been subconsciously considering my suggestion?'

Nothing subconscious about where her mind had been. 'What suggestion? Sorry, haven't given it a thought.' Heat was spreading over her neck and even in the air conditioning she felt her T-shirt sticking to her skin. 'Pookie's just a little white rabbit with wings...'

'Is he?' He smiled and sliced off another piece of mango but she could tell he thought she was making up one of her fairy stories.

'Yes. He is. Was. It was my favourite storybook when I was young and... I'm going to take one of the hotel's famous rain showers before we head out.' In that luxury shower room big enough for an entire football team. Or one blue-eyed golden man. She caught his hopeful look as she stood up, and shook her head. 'Don't even think about it.'

'Can't stop a man thinking,' she heard him say as she walked away.

A couple of hours later, they were wandering the narrow alleyways of the textile souq with its shuttered shops and rainbows of colourful silks and exotic fabrics. Everything from jewelled Arabian slippers to belly-dancing costumes to the latest fashion in business suits.

Desert heat and unfamiliar scents and a lone Arabic voice chanting prayerfully assaulted Chloe's senses. Tourists and locals in Western dress rubbed shoulder to shoulder with those in more traditional clothing.

She chose a couple of skeins of silken fabric for the simple reason that she couldn't imagine leaving Dubai without them, so Jordan insisted she visit one of the resident tailors and have something made up while they were there. He offered extra cash for the garments to be constructed and delivered to the hotel by the end of the day.

'But you paid me already,' she told him, feeling awkward about the expense. 'I'd not have bought it if I'd known. I pay my own way.'

'Not this time. I want you to play the role you've accepted, and play it well. My wife's wish is my command.'

Jordan was a proud man and she knew his tone well enough not to argue about it for now.

So Chloe made it her Pretty Woman adventure. But it didn't end with the textile souq; it was on to the Burjuman Centre with its high-end fashion labels where she purchased off-the-rack garments. Business attire for their meetings and attractive, modest casual-wear.

And one of the best surprises she discovered was that shopping with a man could actually be fun. Well, shopping with Jordan was fun. He had a good eye for women's fashion; little wonder with the gorgeous types she'd seen draped on his arm in the media pictures. He was protective of her when he saw other men, even women, staring at her blonde hair as if she were some sort of curiosity. And the way he looked at her every time she modelled something for his advice or approval…well, it was…flattering.

More than flattering. It was hot. And she hadn't felt the kind of hot Jordan made her feel in a long time. The kind that spread like nettle rash over sensitised skin. The kind that made you itch and burn and yearn for something to ease and soothe.

And he knew it.

He was playing the role of adoring, indulgent husband to the hilt. His not-so-subtle, underhanded way to lure her with the promised pleasures of afternoon delights didn't faze her, oh, no.

It only cemented her decision to maintain that professional distance. Men like him were far too sure of themselves, and she was getting in over her head with this one. That yearning ache was a reminder of her vulnerability where relationships were concerned. Any relationship.

I don't fit in.

After this charade was over and done they'd go their separate ways because what would a millionaire gold-mining magnate want with a short-stack wandering adventurer like her? *Walk away first.*

So after lunch in one of the mall's shaded courtyards, when Jordan suggested—with a twinkle in his blue eyes—that they return to the hotel because he had business to catch up on, Chloe stayed in town to do some exploring on her own.

Jordan closed down his laptop and scowled at the magnificent ocean view from the suite's magnificent gold-and-mahogany desk. He hadn't expected to end up spending the rest of the afternoon on his own. His suggestion to return to the hotel had been business motivated—he *had* left Australia sooner than he'd anticipated, sending his PA into a spin—but not entirely. He'd hoped Chloe would have accompanied him back here, given the looks they'd exchanged while she'd modelled some of the world's great fashion labels for him.

Contrary Chloe. He couldn't remember a time when a woman had held out for so long, given the obvious attraction. There was something about anticipation that heightened the senses, but it came with an impatience that staccato-tapped up and down his spine.

His phone buzzed on the desk and he reached for it with a grin—not so long after all. 'Miss me already, Blondie?'

'Mr Blackstone?' The unfamiliar Arabic-accented male voice brought Jordan crashing down.

Hell and damn. 'Yes—*na'an.* I apologise, sir, I was expecting Chl—my wife to call.' Jordan reined in his sudden tension and tried to remember the Arabic he'd learned for the trip. '*Marhaba.* How can I help you?'

'*Marhabtayn.* I am calling on behalf of Sheikh Qasim bin Omar Al-Zeid.'

Jordan straightened, his fingers tightening on the phone. 'Yes?' His voice came out clipped and terse.

'Sheikh Qasim will not be able to meet with you tomorrow as planned. A family emergency has occurred. He will be in contact soon. Meanwhile he sends his apologies and would have you accept a special gift instead. You are on your honeymoon, *na'an*?'

'*Na'an.*'

'Please be ready to depart on the helipad of your hotel with your wife at noon tomorrow. It will be an overnight stay, so you may want to bring any essential items with you.'

'*Shukran.* That's very generous. Please convey my thoughts regarding his family and my gratitude to Sheikh Qasim on behalf of myself and my wife.'

The words 'my wife' felt strange and foreign on his lips but Jordan shook off the odd discomfort and disconnected with a smile. His would-be business partner had not changed his mind as Jordan had briefly feared. He'd given a show of faith and arranged something special for their honeymoon.

Pushing up from the desk, he punched the air and thanked whatever good luck demon had been riding on his shoulder when he'd decided an accompanying 'wife' would be a clever tactical move.

Meanwhile, he had a surprise evening of his own to plan,

which included sand, sea and celestial sights. He walked to the bathroom to shower and change before Chloe returned. Sex might also be on the agenda if he played his cards right.

But his anticipation in sharing the evening with his woman of the moment was marred somewhat when he recalled his sheer stupidity in answering a call without checking caller ID. He *never* answered without checking caller ID. Thoughtful, he narrowed his gaze as he stripped off and stepped under the spray. Was his fascination with Chloe interfering with his work?

No. Fascination equated to captivation, which implied a weakness on his part. That he wasn't in full control, that Chloe wielded some sort of power over him. Switching the spray to cold—and full power—he let it pummel his back and assured himself what he felt was lust. Honest to goodness lust.

And women did *not* interfere with his work. This small blip was nothing to worry about. It was just his pent-up libido demanding action. He set the lather to his hair and worked his fingers hard. Soon everything would return to normal. It would all settle down once they'd had sex. Then he could focus on what he'd come to Dubai to do.

CHAPTER EIGHT

'I'M GOING TO knock your socks off tonight, husband of mine,' Chloe announced when she returned late in the afternoon with purchases trailing behind her, carried by staff who discreetly disappeared as soon as they'd set the bags down. 'At least I hope I am.'

He was rather hoping she'd be knocking—or, rather, *taking*—more than his socks off. When she plonked herself on the nearest brocade chair, kicked off her shoes and massaged a foot, he couldn't help but notice the slender shape of her ankle. His groin tightened. He wanted to put his hands there. His mouth. He wanted to kiss his way over that sexy arched instep and up her calf. Her thigh. All the way to paradise... 'Let me do that for you.'

He half rose but she shook her head and waved him away, hugging one knee to her chest, whisky eyes flashing a warning. 'Uh-uh. You do *not* want to smell my feet after a day in the desert.'

He grinned. There was that. 'Okay. Later maybe.'

She didn't look at him, chin resting on her knee as she squeezed and flexed her foot. 'I'm going to need an hour to get ready for this romantic dinner package you arranged for your devoted wife, and you need to be somewhere else while I do.'

'Ah, a little mystery, I like that in a relationship. Keeps it alive, wouldn't you agree?'

'No.' She yanked the band from her hair and shook it out like a cloud of curly sunshine but thunder darkened her expression. A moment later she shrugged and lost some of that vehemence as she met his eyes and acknowledged, 'It depends on the mystery.'

'And the man. Don't let one bad experience with a Mr Despicable spoil everything for you, Chloe,' he told her softly.

'Jordan...' She stopped, then said slowly, 'Mr Despicable hasn't spoiled everything.'

'Glad to hear it.' As she turned away to fiddle with her hair he got the distinct feeling Despicable wasn't the only man who'd hurt her.

Grabbing his suit jacket and a tie, he went downstairs to wander the plethora of fountains and gardens in the hotel complex before heading back to the lobby to wait.

Chloe appeared punctually at the top of the escalator as arranged. And taking his breath away in a long, loose sheath that flowed like an emerald river to her feet where shimmering amethyst sandals peeked beneath the hem. An embroidered purse no bigger than a CD and suspended on black silk rope hung on her shoulder. Everything about her was casually elegant and perfect for intimate dining on the water's edge.

Even as she descended he could smell her skin, as if she'd soaked in a bath of jasmine, then been dusted with golden cinnamon. Her hair was scrunched in a tortoiseshell clip on top of her head, and as she reached him he had to restrain himself from burying his nose against her neck and filling his hands with her sweet flesh. *No PDAs, Blackstone, remember?*

He stuck his hands in his trouser pockets instead and said, 'Consider me sockless.'

Her smile danced across her features, topaz eyes reflecting the setting sun's brilliance a thousandfold. 'Thank you. And you look pretty snappy too, as usual.'

He held out his arm. 'Shall we?'

'We shall.' She tucked her hand around his elbow, her wedding ring glinting. 'Such a glorious evening.'

'And it's only just begun.'

She flicked him a glance from beneath her lashes but didn't reply. At least she hadn't shattered his vision and hopes yet.

They walked the short distance to their reserved table. The romantic package lived up to its name with crisp white-covered chairs protected from the sand by a Persian carpet, Moroccan brass lanterns, the scent of incense on the marine air mingling with the delicate tropical blooms on the cloth-topped table. Gleaming gold cutlery, sparkling crystal.

And Chloe.

'Does your friend Sadiq know about this arrangement between us?' she asked when they'd ordered their meal and toasted the evening with one of his favourite Australian whites, chilled and fizzing to perfection.

'He knows you accompanied me. What about you? Have you told your family yet?'

She shook her head, then sipped again, thoughtful. 'Maybe I should. Then when we go home we could…'

We. The word speared through him—not a word he wanted to hear in the context of home and family—and his muscles tensed.

Then she sighed, her gaze focused inward. 'No. That wouldn't work.'

He dared ask, 'What were you thinking?'

She barely flicked a hand and he glimpsed something in her eyes—defeat or resignation? 'Nothing sensible, that's for sure.' Straightening, she set her glass on the table with a decisive *plunk*. 'I've deposited ample funds in their account, so now I'm thinking maybe I'll stay on in Melbourne for a bit, work for Dana. Who knows? They don't need to know I'm back in Australia just yet.'

'You wouldn't go see them?'

'Why? I'm their mistake. I *am* a mistake.' She spoke matter-of-factly, no malice, no anger. 'The "clever" genes had run out by the time I was conceived.'

Jordan frowned, angry on her behalf that her parents and even her siblings had made her feel she was worthless in their eyes. At the same time he understood where she was coming from because Ina had also blamed him for being born and punished him for it every day of his young life.

In Jordan's eyes, Chloe owed her family nothing. 'Why would you want to bail them out?'

'Because whoever they are, whatever they've done or not done, they're family.' She looked at him, honest eyes reflecting the vermilion hues of sunset. 'I know you understand. This trip, your goal here in Dubai, is about family.'

He couldn't respond to that because what she said was true. And it wasn't as if his dad had been perfect. Far from it. The man could've done much more for Jordan as a child. He could've been a stronger father and banished Ina from their lives years ago instead of turning a blind eye for love. Because Dad had loved his cheating wife more than he'd loved his only son.

Love makes you weak.

He shook it away. With the lavender sky tossing up flames of scarlet and purple, the air thick with barbecued meats and spices, the sound of water lapping lazily on the sand, not to mention the company of an attractive and interesting woman, he refused to let the past crowd in on the present.

He tilted his glass towards her. 'Tonight's not about family, Blondie. It's about us.'

They sampled each other's dishes. Moroccan chicken with orange and cinnamon tagine, and Syrian flame-grilled kafta kebabs with sour cherry sauce on pitta bread and topped with pine nuts.

Jordan found Chloe an intelligent and stimulating conversationalist who wasn't afraid to challenge or even disagree with his views, unlike so many of his dates who went along with whatever he said, testing the limits of his boredom.

They shared a double chocolate ice-cream fantasy as the blaze of sunset surrendered to the deep purple of evening and the stars blinked on and the air cooled. A waxing moon hung like a misshapen pearl in the sky.

Chloe rested her elbows on the cleared table and stared up at its cold ethereal beauty. No matter where she went in a sometimes unfamiliar world, the moon was a constant. 'I could watch that pretty ball for hours,' she said. 'First an amazing sunset, now this.'

'I did promise you celestial sights.'

'Oh?' Her brow lifted. 'I think I missed that memo.'

'Maybe I forgot to mention it.' He rose, shrugged off his suit jacket, slung it over his shoulder and took her hand loosely in his. 'Let's walk. I want to show you something.' She slipped off her shoes and he led her onto the sand, away from the glare. He stood behind her and pointed to two bright celestial objects in the west and close together. 'That's Venus and Jupiter.'

'Uh-huh.' She knew her way around the night sky too, loved the changing panorama the different hemispheres brought, but she'd never found it quite as exciting with Jordan standing behind, their bodies not quite touching, his deep voice rumbling by her ear.

The wine in her system had blurred the line she'd promised herself she wouldn't cross and she turned her head and stared up at his face. Moonlight carved hills and valleys into his strong features and for a moment their gazes meshed in

silence while the marine breeze blew gently across her skin
and the water slapped on the beach.

'So…where's the Big Dipper?' she asked, all innocence—
buying into his game.

'Over here. See that star just above that palm…?' With
light hands, he shifted her position—as she knew he would—
so that she was facing a more northerly direction, and his right
arm lifted in front of her. She smelled soap and fresh cotton
and tempting man, and her body started to quiver.

He traced the shape in the air for her. 'You can't see it
from Australia.'

'But we can see the three brightest stars in the sky, and
the Southern Cross is by far my favourite constellation.' She
turned so that she faced him fully, taking a step away to see
him better. 'And Saturn is visible in the morning this month.
Near the Pleiades.'

His grin was slow and wide. 'You had me fooled for a
moment.'

She grinned back. 'I did.'

His eyes took on a molten silver glint. 'And this is payback
time where I haul you into my arms and kiss you senseless.'
Except he didn't.

'And I let you,' she murmured, melting fast beneath his
gaze. 'But that's not going to happen. We're not on Bondi
Beach now.'

'I wouldn't do what I want to do to you on a public beach,
Blondie.' His gaze flicked to her feet, then strolled all the
way up her body to her eyes. 'I'd take you to a very private
place where, short of a tsunami, no one and nothing would
interrupt us for a very long time.'

Her nipples tightened viciously in the wake of his leisurely perusal. She knew she shouldn't poke a tiger but she
returned the favour, giving her gaze permission to slow when
it reached the suspicious outline of a bulge in his dark trou-

sers. She was safe here with people not far away—not only from him, but from herself. 'And what would you do in this private place? Theoretically.'

His jaw firmed, his eyes sparking like a welder's blowtorch. 'Come here.'

'Come? Here?' She glanced around them and stifled a naughty giggle. '*Here's* going to get you in a lot of trouble—'

'Us,' he said, his voice tight. 'It's going to get *us* in trouble. Follow me.' He set a fast pace across the sand towards a row of luxury recliner chairs on a deck a short distance from the tables where diners were still enjoying their meals.

Jordan had coupled them in a sexual context, sending a thrill zipping down her spine. Shoes dangling from one hand and her feet tripping over themselves in the sand, she followed.

On the decking, he stopped and turned around. Smouldering desire in the eyes that captured hers. For a guy who worked out, his breathing was on the fast and shallow side, drawing Chloe's attention to his chest as he dragged in air. Her fingers itched to touch, to get to work between those buttons—

He tossed his jacket down, unbuttoned the top button of his shirt and loosened his tie with swift sharp movements. 'You want to know what I'd do and I'm going to tell you. Right here. Right now.'

He sat on the side of a recliner with his shiny black shoes on the ground, and gestured for her to sit facing him on the recliner next to his as if they reflected one another in a mirror. His knees were a hand-span from hers, their torsos within touching distance, but he didn't reach for her, nor did she for him. To anyone passing by they looked like a respectable couple discussing the weather.

'Place your hands on the chair either side of your thighs,'

Jordan said. 'Move them back a bit, so you're leaning back slightly and I can see the shape of your breasts.'

Her nipples responded instantly to his request, tight buds pressing against her bra as she followed his instruction.

'Spread your legs a bit—not too much—just enough room for my hand to fit between.' He must have glimpsed her alarm because he said, 'Don't worry, this is sex without touching.'

'Like phone sex?' She did as he asked, her loose ankle-length dress hiding any hint of impropriety. To any passer-by she looked as if she was perfectly relaxed and admiring the moon. And she told herself she was—relaxed and totally in control.

'Better than phone sex because I can see you.' His voice rolled over her like honey. 'I can smell you. I can watch your responses and know I'm turning you on.'

For all she knew, he might have been complimenting her perfume, but the earthiness of the image that spun through her mind's eye was as intimate as it was shocking and a surge of liquid heat pooled low in her belly.

'I'm turning you on already.' He cocked his head to one side, studying her. 'Your breath caught and your eyes have gone wide and dark. What were you thinking about?'

No, he most definitely hadn't been talking about her choice in perfume. 'If I tell you, where's the mystery?' She squirmed on the seat and cleared the lust frog from her throat. 'Is this going to be all about me or do I get to return the favour?'

'All about you, Blondie.' He waved away her attempt to turn the tables. 'Your hair's gorgeous, even at night, but you need to let it down. So I'm removing that torture clip.' He gestured with a hand. 'You could do that for me.'

'I could, but…' Blue eyes mesmerised and entranced and the rest of her sentence trailed away forgotten. She freed her hair and finger-combed it so that it drifted down around her shoulders.

He nodded. 'That's a relief, right? All that tension in the scalp draining away.'

How did he know? she wondered. Of course the answer was obvious—he knew women. He knew what they liked, what they wanted. And he knew how to give it to them.

'I'm massaging my fingertips against your scalp,' he continued. 'You used the hotel's shampoo—I can smell peaches.'

Yes. She closed her eyes. To concentrate on his voice or to shut out that piercing gaze that suddenly seemed to know her too well? Maybe she wasn't as in control as she'd thought.

'Under the stars your hair looks like milk and feels like satin. I'm caressing your throat with light fingers. Smooth, like china. My lips are there now, where your pulse is galloping with anticipation. I'm lapping your sweetness while my hands slip around and lower your zip, my knuckles grazing every vertebra until I reach the base of your spine. Bra hooks next. I draw the dress and bra from your shoulders. Down your arms in one slow stroke. The heat from your skin rises to my nostrils, bringing your scent. Oriental spices. Jasmine. Arousal. Open your eyes, Chloe. Look into my eyes and see what you do to me.'

What she saw in those sparkling blues made her whole body limp. What she heard in his voice stroked her insides with a silken glove. Desire, heat, arousal, anticipation. And she felt like a kitten, arching her head against that touch.

He nodded. 'And I do the same to you.'

'Yes…' Her voice trailed away on a wisp of night breeze, to hang around the stars that seemed to be slowly spinning overhead like a kaleidoscope.

'Don't look away again.' His command was low and firm. 'I've been imagining your breasts since that first night you had them stuffed into that too-tight costume.' Greedy eyes stroked her bodice. 'Washed with moonshine, they're firm and luscious with nipples the colour of…a watermelon smoothie,' he decided. 'And they taste like pink champagne.'

Her blood fizzed, the sound almost shattering her ear-drums. 'Jordan…stop…' She tried to look beyond him and focus on the inky splashed silver beach, the moonlit curve of the Arabian tower against a black velvet sky, and get herself in order, but the powerful lure of his voice dragged her back.

'You don't mean that,' he murmured, low and sure and seductive. 'Can you feel the pull of my tongue as I draw one nipple inside my mouth and tease it with my teeth while I tweak the other between my fingers?'

Her nipples cramped; pleasure in the pain as she arched her back, craving more. 'Jordan…please…'

'Since you asked so nicely…' Humour and playfulness in his voice.

So powerful, so intense, Chloe swore she felt him swap breasts. Moist heat fanned her skin as if he were breathing against her décolletage and she couldn't tell if the slippery abrading sensation was her clothing or her vivid imagination.

'I'm taking their weight in my hands now and blowing on the wetness.'

His voice was dreamlike in the stillness of the evening, emptying her mind while he filled her with image upon image, sensation upon sensation. 'I…I think that's enough…'

He shook his head once, his eyes like blue lasers in the dimness. 'I'm just getting started.' He stroked her knees with those eyes and she wondered if he could see them tremble. 'Relax and let me touch you. My hand's gliding up over your thighs, an inch at a time, spinning out the anticipation. They're a little flushed and feel incredible, like you bathed in rose petals and cherry liqueur. My fingers reach the edge of your panties. Can you feel the heat?' His eyes drew her inside him. 'I can.'

'Jordan…I need… We need—'

'Yes. I know.' He smiled. 'That control you had earlier has melted away like an ice-cream sundae under an Arabian sun, hasn't it?' It wasn't a question.

No. Yes... She rolled her lips together as moisture pooled between her legs, ready for him. So ready...

'You sigh and shift your legs farther apart and my thumb finds you slick and wet and hot. Do you feel hot, Blondie?'

Her eyelids fluttered down as she shifted on the recliner. 'Yes...'

'Here? Where I'm letting the tips of my fingers glide? Or here, where my mouth is lapping at your neck. Or maybe—'

'Hot,' she moaned. 'Everywhere.'

'That ripping sound is me tearing that scrap of silk from your hips, dragging it out of the way so I can slide one finger inside you. One's not enough for you, is it? You want more. Spread your legs wider—I want to see all of you.'

Her eyes snapped open and met his and just like that she complied, her long skirt dipping into the V between her thighs. 'See all of me,' she murmured. 'Touch me.' Her voice lowered to a husky whisper and she tossed caution to the wind. 'Taste me.'

His eyes turned black, a muscle jumped in his cheek and his knuckles turned white on the edge of the recliner. 'Y—'

His mobile ringtone shattered the fantasy. Chloe jumped like a guilty thirteen-year-old caught behind the bike shed with the school's bad boy. For a moment neither moved, nor spoke, staring at each other while the beat of some rap tune jiggled and vibrated in his trouser pocket.

She bit her lips together. *Don't answer it.*

He pulled the offending object out, glanced at the screen then back to Chloe, the spark in his eyes doused but not extinguished. 'I have to answer this.' He rose, explaining, 'It's my PA,' and already walking away into the nearby shadows. 'Roma. What's the problem?'

He halted at some potted tropical plants. Chloe couldn't hear the words but he spoke in short, sharp sentences, his movements jerky and impatient, indicating a problem, possibly urgent.

Her whole body wailed in protest as she threw a glance up at the night sky. As if she didn't have an urgent problem herself—one that needed his immediate and undivided attention.

A breeze blew off the water, cooling her flushed skin, and she counted to ten. It was enough to clear the sensual fog that had enshrouded her, and she rubbed her upper arms with brisk movements. She needed to think, which wasn't easy when her brain cells were melting from an overload of X-rated images.

She turned away from the sight of the man responsible and watched the water lap against the sand. *Pull yourself together, Chloe Montgomery. Take back that control you were so proud of and walk away. Now.*

Because obviously the social part of the evening was over and it was just as well because another moment and she'd have been begging him to take her to their room and finish what he'd started. Worse, he knew it.

She'd been about to allow a man to override her decisions. Again. It was still a raw gash; how easily Markos had persuaded her into bed that night and to part with what little money she'd had. How he'd played her body like a piano while convincing her that he knew the financial markets and could triple her money in a week. *Trust me, Chloe.*

'Chloe.'

She swivelled on one heel, her arms across her chest. She didn't dare look directly at the gorgeous man in front of her who was her *business* partner. 'I'm heading up to the room now,' she clipped. 'Don't try anything because I've already made it clear I will not compromise our business relationship. *You* may be able to switch—'

'That was a call from Perth.' The tension in his voice drew her attention as he walked towards her. 'There's a problem at one of the mines.'

CHAPTER NINE

'Oh, no.' Their fantasy vanished like moon dust down a black hole. A mine emergency could change everything they'd come here to do. 'Is it serious?'

'No one seems to know yet.'

'Is there anything I can do? Would you like me to wait with you till you find out?'

He was too busy on his mobile to look at her, the screen casting a pale glow across the grim slash of his mouth. 'Not your problem, Chloe. Go on up to the room.'

'But I… You might…' She trailed off. The man was in no need of her assistance. The tone, the body language clearly told her he didn't want her here. 'If you change your mind…'

He glanced her way as if suddenly remembering he had a dinner companion. A wife. 'I'll escort you up, then I have to make some calls, find out what the hell's going on. I'll do that down here or in the lobby.'

'Please…' Chloe gave a half-laugh '…I can find my own way.'

'I said I'll see you up.'

'No. I'd prefer you didn't.' She touched his arm lightly. 'Stay and make your calls. I'm perfectly safe and you're busy.' She stepped away. 'Just remember I'm here if you need someone.'

'Right…'

She didn't exist to him and she turned away, pointed herself in the direction of the hotel and didn't look back. She didn't know why he'd opted not to avail himself of the luxurious office in their suite to make his calls. After what had just happened between them, perhaps he needed space and privacy to get on with the job. No distractions. Perhaps he thought *she* did.

Or perhaps he was more like her than she'd imagined—used to doing everything on his own. Except that he did so by choice whereas she'd learned through necessity.

Some instinct whispered that maybe it hadn't always been his choice either, and as soon as she reached their suite she opened her laptop and logged on to the internet. She'd seen something so sad, so haunted in his eyes when they'd spoken of family. Up till now, she'd refrained from learning more about the man than was necessary for the job requirement, but his expression earlier this evening had aroused her curiosity.

She found an article on his charity. Rapper One was a fund he'd set up that took troubled teenage boys from broken homes and situations of neglect into the bush for some team-building and adventure every six months. He didn't stop at fund-raising. He hired the services of counsellors and psychologists and mentored these kids personally, teaching them how to pan for gold while building trust and self-esteem amongst the group.

There was so much more she wanted to know, but tonight was about being here for him if there was bad news and he needed someone to talk to. She closed the computer and prepared to wait up.

Jordan dragged off his tie and swiped a hand over his hair, willing his phone to ring, waiting for word and feeling so helpless. What the hell was happening on the other side of the world? If he didn't hear something soon, he—*they*—would be on tomorrow's first flight to Australia. He needed to be there; his mine, his responsibility. Was it some safety issue he'd not addressed? Some management concern he'd overlooked?

At the first flicker of life, Jordan stabbed the answer button, barked, 'What's going on?' then listened as relief poured through him. Seemed there wasn't a problem after all. It had been a misunderstanding. A couple of miners they'd thought missing underground had turned up safe and well. Very sorry to have troubled him, to have worried him. *Enjoy the rest of your trip.*

He swore long and hard as he disconnected—even though it was the best outcome possible—and headed to one of the empty tables, ordered a double Scotch, no ice, from the waiter who appeared at his side.

He glared at the recliner chairs where he'd last seen Chloe and his jaw tightened. He'd almost chosen not to answer his phone because he'd been too focused on the red-hot blonde all but coming apart in front of him. He'd been tempted to put a woman before his work. The repercussions of that choice echoed with eerie familiarity.

Eight years ago he'd allowed a woman he barely knew to persuade him to 'stay a little longer'. He'd missed his flight and his father had died that day. He'd put personal desires before what was important in his life.

And then there'd been Lynette. He'd been willing to put her first without question until he'd learned she'd been using his feelings for her all along.

The waiter placed his crystal tumbler on the table. Jordan thanked him and raised it to eye-level. *The colour of Chloe's eyes*—ah, yes, she'd made damn sure he'd never forget her, with that whisky gaze of hers, hadn't she? He downed the contents in one go, needing its full-bodied burn as it slid down his throat.

Women manipulated.

But tonight, he had to admit that generalisation wasn't fair. This evening with Chloe, he'd been the one doing the manipulating. He'd known precisely what he was doing and where it was leading.

Then when his phone had rung with such incredibly bad timing, had she told him to ignore it like some women he knew would? No, *he'd* been the one telling himself to ignore it. When he'd told her the problem, he'd seen genuine concern and caring in her eyes. She'd put his problems before her own needs or any promise of mutually satisfying pleasure.

And he'd almost been tempted to share the uncertainty, to ask her to wait with him for news, good or bad. The way a husband would with his wife. But he never involved the women he dated in his business concerns. His father was a not-so-shining example of what could happen if you did.

She wasn't a date.

Half an hour later he let himself into their suite and walked straight to the bedroom. Chloe wasn't there but she'd put every available cushion down the centre of the bed. A half-grin hooked the corner of his mouth. If he wanted, he could have her lush little body arching wantonly—and willingly—beneath him in a matter of moments, cushions or no. But it was a symbolic action and he'd respect her decision. He wouldn't even try to change her mind.

Not tonight anyway.

From the corner of his eye he saw movement in the semi-dimness of the adjacent room. Chloe was standing at the window and staring out at the moonlit sea, framed by the structure's white lattice and looking little-girl lost in a too-big sweatshirt that might have been red once but was now a sad pink flecked with grey. 'Chloe.'

She whirled around, anxiety etched on her face, fatigue smudges beneath her eyes. 'What happened? Have you heard?

Is everything okay?' She rapid-fired questions at him as she crossed the gold-brocade-edged carpet towards him.

'Everything's fine. There was no emergency after all.'

She huffed out a breath. 'Well, why the heck didn't they get their facts straight before calling you and worrying you like that when you're so far away? I hope you gave them a piece of your mind.'

Her indignation on his behalf made him smile. 'I expect them to keep me informed with up-to-date info. Maybe they just didn't like the idea of me over here enjoying myself.' The lines bracketing her mouth didn't relax and his smile faded almost before it began. 'I thought you'd be asleep by now.'

Her eyes flashed, concern shifting to annoyance. 'You thought wrong. Did you assume I'd just go to sleep and think nothing of your emergency?' She shoved her hands into her hair, making it stand up like a wild halo. 'Of course I waited up. You wouldn't let me wait with you but that didn't stop me from worrying right along with you anyway.'

He frowned. His assumptions had been way off, and something vaguely disquieting skittered down his spine. He fiddled with his shirt cuffs, slid the buttons free. 'I didn't expect you to do that. I *don't* expect you to do that.'

'Isn't that what a good wife would do?' she demanded, a fire in her eyes that twisted something inside him. 'Wouldn't she be there to support her husband anyway she can?'

'I didn't pay you to be involved in my business problems, Chloe.'

Rather than soothe that fire, it inflamed. '*Pay* me,' she repeated, tersely. 'You *paid* me to be your wife. I don't know why but you make it sound cheap. You make this whole arrangement sound cheap.' She flicked her hand and her ten-thousand-dollar wedding ring glinted in the half-light.

He raised a brow but not his voice. 'That's not my intention since this *whole arrangement's* costing me a great deal of money.' *Keep emotion out of it; stick to the facts.* 'You're tired, Chloe. Go to bed.'

'I intend to.' She walked past him then stopped and met his gaze full on. 'For the record, I wasn't worried because you were paying me to be worried. I happen to care.'

Her words struck him like a velvet fist mid-chest. He started unbuttoning his shirt. 'That's not necessary,' he bit out. *Care* was not a part of their deal.

'So sue me for breach of contract,' she tossed back, and climbed into bed.

Hell. He didn't answer because for once in his life he didn't know how to respond. He suspected that any further conversation at this point wouldn't end well, and he could allow nothing to jeopardise their agreement.

He told himself her disposition would perk up with tomorrow's getaway, which he'd surprise her with over breakfast. And he'd do what he knew how to do best. She'd return to Dubai refreshed and satisfied, her cheeks bright with a lover's glow, her eyes sparkling.

And the deal with the Dubai gold buyer would be in the bag.

Chloe dragged the heaven-soft quilt over her shoulders and lay stiff and tense and facing away from Jordan's side of the bed. Clearly, he didn't want her involved in his personal life. She'd been *paid* to be his wife. But not a wife who mattered in the great scheme of things. Not a wife who could be a support if he'd let her.

Not even a friend or someone to confide in.

She closed her eyes. But her ears were working fine. Too fine. She heard the shoosh of fabric shifting over all that golden skin as he removed his shirt, the clink of his belt buckle, the *zzzz* of a zip as he shucked off his trousers...

Was he still wearing underwear or was he going to get into

bed naked? She'd lay bets on the latter because that was the type of man he was—arrogant and cocky where women were concerned. Especially the women sharing his bed.

If she wanted, she could roll over and see if the reality lived up to her vivid imagination, and—no doubt in her mind—he was counting on her to do just that. She squeezed her eyes tighter and wished she'd thought to bring earplugs because he sounded as if he was scratching...somewhere. She did *not* want to know.

There was a slight disturbance in the air as he slid beneath the quilt but the mattress remained as still as a lake at sunset, and almost as wide. With the Great Dividing Range between.

She'd half expected him to sweet-talk her into finishing what they'd started but she didn't hear so much as a murmur. Was he waiting for her to make the move? *It'll be you inviting me.* His words echoed in her head.

Her body was still wide awake and tingling and he hadn't laid a hand on her. Imagine what the real deal would be like... The residual heat between her thighs intensified once more and spread to every yearning and unfulfilled place he'd awoken with nothing more than his voice and eyes.

She pressed her lips together to stifle a moan and forced her restless legs to remain still. She only had to slide across the silky lake, climb over the mountain range and she could live the fantasy for real.

She feared it was only a matter of time before Jordan's charisma and smooth talking overcame her resistance. And worse, much worse, it wasn't only his charm that she was falling for, it was the man. He'd been fun today, a great sightseeing companion, good-humoured and patient while she'd trawled the fashion boutiques. He was also a man who took responsibility seriously, cared for his staff and troubled teens.

But it would be a dangerous mistake to let him close. So she would fight him and his charms with every ounce of will power she had.

When Jordan surfaced from a disturbed sleep interrupted by erotic dreams, Chloe's side of the bed was empty. Which was just as well, he decided, all things considered. He could smell her fresh-from-the-shower scent overlaid with the equally enticing aroma of a full English breakfast.

Pulling his jeans on over his boxers—not an easy task in his state—he followed his nose in search of the coffee pot. He found Chloe sitting at the breakfast table flicking through sightseeing brochures. She'd tied her hair back and he approved the conservative elbow-sleeved navy dress that met Dubai's fashion etiquette. 'Good morning.'

She looked up, her eyes instantly drawn to his chest, then quickly looked back to her reading material. 'Good morning.' She waved a hand at the table and said, 'I didn't know what you liked so I ordered everything.'

'Everything.' His eyes roamed over the sea of silver domes on the table and he had to grin. It appeared she was serious.

'The staff were waiting to serve you but I sent them away… I didn't know what time you'd be getting up.'

He stepped up to the table. 'And you wanted to make sure you wouldn't still be in bed when I did.'

Bingo. Chloe felt the blush explode into her cheeks. She lowered her head farther and reached for another pamphlet. 'I…I'm an early riser.'

'So am I,' he murmured, all lazy innuendo. The tips of her ears burned like a furnace, and she felt him lean in so that his lips grazed one to whisper, 'Why didn't you wake me?'

Honey over sand. Her breath caught, her pulse blipped. That sleep-husky voice was a reminder of last night and how she'd come so close to losing control, and in the glaring light of day she felt the flames of embarrassment all the way to her toes.

She gritted her teeth and decided a women's-only spa session was on this morning's agenda. Maybe she could make it last all day. 'We both know the reason for that.'

'I wonder if it'll still hold true for tomorrow?' Thankfully, he moved away, lifting domes and piling a plate with bacon and eggs. 'You've eaten, then.'

'Yes.' She replayed his words in her head then turned, studying him with narrowed eyes. 'Tomorrow morning won't be any different.'

He looked far too smug as he poured himself a coffee. 'Ah, yes, it will. Because tonight, Mrs Blackstone, we're to be treated to an Arabian honeymoon special, courtesy of Sheikh Qasim.'

Her heart thumped once, hard. 'What?'

'The sheikh's had some family emergency. It's an apology for postponing our meeting.'

'Postponing?' Chloe stared at him, a spurt of panic trickling through her bloodstream. 'How long for?'

'I don't know yet. I'm sure we'll hear very soon.' He smiled—a hint of wicked fun—over the gold rim of his cup. 'Don't look so worried.'

That devil's smile was supposed to reassure? 'So what's this honeymoon special we're being treated to?' More importantly, what did it involve and how did it impact on her decision to keep that space between them?

'It's a magical mystery tour for me too. We have to be ready with an overnight bag by noon.'

All night. Just the two of them in some romantic getaway spot? This wasn't good. She shook her head. 'You go. I… have a salon appointment this afternoon.'

His eyes cooled, as rapidly as molten steel turned black

when dropped in water, and a muscle tensed in his jaw. 'Then cancel it.'

His reaction and demand stunned her. She'd never heard him speak that way to her and shock curdled with something akin to fear beneath her breastbone. That loss of control feeling reminded her of Markos and the subtle but dangerous power he'd had over her. It was her worst nightmare and she struggled against it. 'I...don't want to cancel.'

His expression hardened further, the lines around his mouth deep, drawn. He set his cup down with a snap. 'Have you forgotten why you're here?'

'No.' She lifted her chin, determined not to let him forget either. 'And it's not to please you in bed.'

Something in his eyes warned her she'd overstepped some boundary. 'You're here as my wife.' He wasn't the smooth charmer now; he was all sharp spikes and business. 'This is our honeymoon and we're going to smile and act like honeymooners.' His jaw was tight. 'For our host at least.'

'But our host won't—'

'His *staff*, Chloe.' His eyes pinned her in place, his warning as clear as thunder over water. 'The status of your bank balance is testament to our *new and happy marriage*.'

'Yes...fine. Okay.' She gulped, embarrassed and humiliated that he'd had to point it out, then nodded. He was right, of course. All the way right. And Jordan had every one of those rights to point out his expectations and her responsibilities. She was glad this incident had happened because for a time there she'd lost focus on the real reason she was in Dubai with Mr Blackstone, gold-mining magnate.

And relieved because now there was no way he'd want anything to do with her beyond their written agreement. He thought she'd tried to weasel her way out of it because she had a nice deposit in her bank account. His opinion of her would be rock-bottom.

He wouldn't know why she'd said what she had—that she was afraid of her developing feelings and her increasing vulnerability. That the more time they spent together was increasingly dangerous. Let him think she was someone who couldn't keep her promises. As agreed, she'd play the part of happy honeymooner for an audience, but anything more wasn't going to happen.

CHAPTER TEN

IT WAS A quiet, awkward morning, both keeping out of the other's way as they packed for their overnight stay. Jordan informed her he had to leave the hotel for a while and asked if she needed anything while he was out. She politely told him she was fine and continued to pack, relieved she had some breathing space on her own.

The helicopter arrived right on time. The pilot soon had their bags stowed and explained their journey would take thirty minutes, travelling along the coast. Chloe had never flown in a helicopter and she compared it to a magic carpet ride as they lifted off the helipad, the Arabian tower growing rapidly smaller as they gained altitude and speed.

Jordan slung an arm around her shoulders, drawing her close and pointing to a ragged group of animals moving across the sand dunes below.

Chloe put aside their differences as his hand pressed against her shoulder, his unique scent filling her nostrils as she leaned over to peer out of his side. 'Camels?'

He nodded. 'A bride's dowry amongst Bedouin tribes.'

She laughed but she wasn't feeling the humour. 'My father would never have had enough camels to get rid of me.'

'I'd have taken you, Blondie,' he assured her, his voice mischievous. 'Even without a camel.' He squeezed her shoulder and she forgot they were acting a part and leaned into him, absorbing the view and simply enjoying his company.

Low grey vegetation dotted the dull red sand dunes as the helicopter began its descent. Trees and date palms came into view followed by a magnificent home that reminded her of a kid's sandcastle. Then they were touching down on a helipad in the middle of a courtyard, surrounded by wide arches leading to cool dark verandas.

A driver on staff met them in a Jeep and introduced himself as Kadar. They were quickly through the huge security gates and bumping over red sand towards nearby dunes.

Two minutes later they topped a rise, a virtual Garden of Eden appeared, the vista spread out before them like a scene from an exotic movie set. A blinding white tent like those used for outdoor weddings had been erected, gauzy curtains at the entrance swirling lazily in the drift of hot desert air. Nearby, water spilled over a rocky outcrop and into a white grotto. A shimmering sapphire and emerald pool reflected lush palms and other vibrant vegetation.

'Oh, wow. It's beautiful,' she breathed.

'And near enough to the coast to take advantage of the sea breeze in the afternoon,' Kadar said, his teeth white against his swarthy complexion as he swung down their bags and carried them towards the tent.

'Come on then, Blondie,' Jordan said, taking her hand. His eyes met hers in shared subterfuge as she climbed out of the vehicle. 'Let's explore our home for the next twenty hours or so.'

The inside of the tent was surprisingly cooler than she'd expected as she removed her sunglasses and stepped past the gauze curtain. Sheer decadence greeted her when her eyes adjusted to the relative dimness. It was more like stepping into a palatial home, or maybe the magical interior of a genie bottle. Low swathes of crimson and purple and gold silks. Plush black sofas arranged around the edge of an intricately designed Persian carpet. Scattered cushions, Moroccan lamps, a bowl of fresh fruit and a bottle of wine chilling in an ice-bucket on a low table.

At the far end a massive four-poster bed covered in black silk with gold and vermilion drapes. Pillows plumped and inviting. Beside her, Jordan reached out and turned her towards him with a smile and a playful eyebrow jiggle. 'A great way to spend a lazy…or not-so-lazy, afternoon.'

Kadar cleared his throat. 'If there is anything you require at any time, a staff member will be at your service. You will use this.' He handed Jordan a communication device. 'Buzz when you are ready for meals.' He gestured to his right. 'The cooler is stocked, there is extra linen. Communication with the outside world is not possible in the tent. If you need to contact anyone I can collect you and take you to the house. The amenities block, when you wish to bathe, is outside to your left.' He glanced at both of them in turn. 'No one will interrupt you here. It is private.'

Jordan squeezed her hand. 'The perfect honeymoon retreat, right, Blondie?' His conspiratorial twinkle had a rippling effect all down her body.

'Couldn't be more perfect. *Pookie.*' She knew Jordan expected her to play along but the word didn't sound as if it was spoken by a loving wife sharing an intimate relationship. It sounded forced. It *was* forced.

If Jordan thought so, he didn't show it. He shook hands with their driver. '*Shukran,* Kadar.'

'Yes,' Chloe agreed. 'This is very kind. Very comfortable. I'm sure we'll enjoy ourselves.'

They stood in the tent's shaded entrance and watched the Jeep disappear over the rise. Remained standing until the sound faded, leaving them with only the splash and trickle of water in the pool, the intermittent sound of an insect in a nearby salt-bush. So quiet she could hear her heart beating. Loudly.

And it was like paradise, the jewelled colours of sky, sand and foliage reflected in the water and dappled sunlight glinting like gold through the palms. If only—

'I've got some business to attend to,' he told her, still watching the sand dunes, that twinkle in his eyes she'd seen earlier gone. He walked to the table where he'd put his briefcase and pulled out a pile of document folders. 'I'm sure a girl like you can entertain herself for a while.' She felt the sudden distance between them like a physical ache.

Arms crossed, she tapped her fingers against her upper arms. 'Too right, I can. I've been doing it all my life.' She was relieved he was going to be too busy to bother with her. His remoteness and lack of interest in sharing this amazing place did *not* disappoint her. It was what she wanted, right? It was totally unnecessary, but she couldn't resist the clipped, 'Don't let me distract you from your work.'

She crossed the room and unzipped her bag, pulled out her swimsuit, a floppy hat and sunscreen. She'd seen an outdoor garden setting beneath the shade of the palms. She'd sit there and read awhile, then cool off in the water. 'Is that little pool safe?'

'Kadar told me it's an underwater spring,' he said, shuffling papers. 'The water's clean if you want to take a dip.' On the table, the intercom buzzed and Jordan reached for it. 'Yes, Kadar…'

Jordan disconnected a moment later, adrenaline zipping around his body. Qasim had left a message at the house to say he was looking forward to meeting Jordan the day after tomorrow. Finally.

He fingered a report he'd requested into mine expansion that he'd been meaning to read since they'd left Australia, then shoved it away. Dammit. He'd told Chloe he had work to do—a lie. What he'd needed was some distance to think about where he'd gone wrong this morning.

His reaction to her plea that he come alone had been swift and vehement and over the top. If he wasn't mistaken, he'd seen fear in her eyes, and despised himself. There was no way he'd have given her a choice, but he'd gone about it all wrong. This tension was his fault.

Pushing up, he paced to the cooler, pulled out a couple of frosty bottles of cola. When did a happy-go-lucky adventurer refuse a free and easy side-trip into the desert?

When it came with conditions—him, for example. But he might never know her reasons because he'd shot first and asked questions later. Actually, he hadn't asked anything at all, he'd simply demanded. And it had spoilt the rapport they'd been building.

He wandered to the tent flap and saw Chloe stretched out on a bench on her stomach, reading a book. Her hat and sunglasses shielded her face so he couldn't tell her mood. Her slim body was poured into a sunny-yellow one-piece, her legs glistening with suntan lotion.

His fingers itched to stroke the backs of those legs, starting at her well-turned ankles and working his way up to those incredibly toned thighs... Blowing out a breath, he wrenched off the top of one of the bottles, drank deeply. Still watching her. Still *imagining*, for God's sake.

She'd had every right to point out that he hadn't paid her to give him pleasure in the bedroom, that it had never been part of their deal. He'd just assumed he could change her mind... His track record with women had made him over-confident.

In two days' time he'd need his focus razor sharp for what was probably the most important deal he'd ever made. The only sure way to clear his mind and give him that focus was to get Chloe out of his system. And he *knew* the attraction wasn't one-sided, that she'd not stop him.

He stepped into the sun and began walking towards her.
He was done watching.
He was done fantasising.

Chloe knew Jordan was approaching. It was as if she'd developed a sixth sense where he was concerned. Her skin got that hot shivery sensation and her heart bopped like a teen at a rock concert. Too late to feign sleep.

And didn't they both want the same thing after all? Wasn't that what all this snapping and tension and tiptoeing around each other was about? Acknowledgement was like fuel adding to the fire singing through her body.

She didn't *want* to acknowledge it. This had to stop—

At the first moist contact, she gasped, then let her breath out slowly as he drew a line of suncream down her spine. 'Stop it.' At least she *thought* it was suncream. Yes, it smelled like suncream. She refused to react. Closing her book, she stood. Her legs felt hot, like melting cheese. The pool looked safe and inviting and she really needed to cool off.

'Hey, Blondie, that needs rubbing in first,' he said behind her.

'You put it there,' she accused, taking off her hat and tossing it on the sand. *Not* turning around. 'You *knew* I'd have to ask you. You did it on *purpose*. That's...*cheating.*'

'I know.' His voice was dark silk with an edge. 'The nice thing about a one-piece is it comes with plenty of bare back.' He punctuated his opinion with a glide of his fingertips along one edge of her swimsuit to the base of her spine.

And so help her, her feet were stuck in the sand. His body heat was a furnace. She could feel it pulling around her like a cloak, drawing them together. 'Rub me, then.' She pressed her lips together before she said any more and cleared that annoying husk from her throat. 'I can hardly go in the pool and leave a trail of white goo...'

'Definitely not.' He sounded amused as he set to work. 'Whatever would our host say?'

'I can't imagine…' She trailed off on a moan. His fingers were firm and skilled and sensuous as they worked from her nape and all the way down. Warm breath tickled the back of her neck and there was a trace of his familiar aftershave in the still air.

'That's enough.' She whirled around to face him, clutching at her elbows to keep from reaching for him and begging him to rub other more sensitive parts that were now throbbing with excruciating intensity. 'I…think that's quite enough. I should be right now.'

He smiled, that big cat gleam in his eyes mesmerising her, holding her captive yet at the same time calling to her to come of her own accord and play the game—a choice, but still his game.

She glanced at the pool—her refuge since he was still fully dressed—and edged towards it. 'You um…have work to do. I won't keep you.'

'Work's over for the day. It's playtime.' He toed off his shoes, began unbuttoning his shirt. He glanced at the table where she saw two bottles of cola. 'Care for a drink before we start?'

Start? 'No, thank you.' She ran the last few steps to the palm-shaded water and slid in feet first, breath catching with the initial shock of hot to cold. When she surfaced, Jordan was gloriously shirtless and pulling off his socks.

She slashed the water from her face and drank in the incredible definition of muscle over bone like a woman too long in the desert. He was a bronzed god, broad shoulders gleaming in the sun, his chest dusted with a smattering of dark hair. Her pulse stuttered and her lungs seemed to be fast running out of oxygen. 'What are you doing?' *Duh*… Not only her lungs, her brain was obviously low on oxygen too.

He unbuckled the belt around his jeans. 'What does it look like?' With a flick of his wrist he unsnapped the stud, revealing a neat little navel and an arrow of hair that pointed to—

'Jordan…' She sank onto a ledge at the edge of the pool, grateful for the water's buoyancy. Her eyes refused to look away from the front of his jeans—it was like being drawn to a car wreck. Which she desperately feared *she'd* be if she didn't slam on the brakes before all control was lost. 'Jordan, don't. I'm serious.'

'So am I.' He grinned. A boy's own, kiss-the-girls-and-make-them-smile kind of grin that would have had schoolgirls running towards him rather than away. His long fingers toyed with the zip. 'Turn around if you don't want to see.'

Turn your back on a predator? She bit her lip. 'You wouldn't…'

Red flag to a bull. As soon as the words were out she realised she'd made a big mistake. The repercussions were already clamouring in her head. 'No. I didn't mean…' She trailed off as he shoved his jeans off, kicked them away.

Temporary relief coursed along her veins. He still wore boxers. Red silk with rearing black stallions…and an impressive tent in front. Oh, good gracious…

Somewhere far overhead she heard the faint sound of a jet on its way somewhere. Progress and technology. Yet here she was in the middle of a desert that probably hadn't changed in thousands of years.

Nor had the attraction between man and woman.

Simple, she thought, *this* man was attracted to *this* woman. And vice versa.

'You're confused, Blondie.'

His richly amused voice reminded her she was still staring at his crotch. 'No, I'm not.'

And she wasn't. Not any more. Her mind was as clear as the ochre horizon. She wanted him. Around her, over her, inside her. All of him. Why pretend otherwise? This attraction wasn't going away and she was through fighting it. Next week she'd deal with the fallout, but next week was a million years away.

'I'm coming in.' Eyes the same colour as the desert sky met hers leaving her in no doubt that he wasn't talking about the pool.

'Thank God,' she murmured.

He didn't look away from her eyes as he walked to the pool and slid into the water so they were both waist-deep...and close. Her heart beat strangely, as if it recognised him and was welcoming him home. But he made no move to touch her. He was waiting for her to make the first move.

'I want you.' She reached out to caress the hard square jaw, then watched her hand travel down the column of his throat, the hard planes of his chest, then over and around tight male nipples. Leaning closer, she pressed a kiss to one, then the other, and heard him groan, felt the strong thump of his heart. She explored his abs, watched his muscles contract beneath her fingers.

Lower, beneath the water's surface until her fingers twisted in the waistband of his boxers. The hard ridge of his erection nudged her hand through the silk and his breath hissed out.

She looked up at him, the tension in his jaw, an unholy fire in his eyes. And murmured, 'Oh, yeah.'

'Chloe.' No teasing pet-name games now, just urgent need and barely leashed control. 'Invite me in.'

'Yes.' She smiled, touched her lips to his briefly and curled herself around him, the heat of his sun-warmed skin a stunning contrast against her water-cooled body.

'Chloe.' His fingers raced over her shoulders and beneath her straps to drag them down her arms so she could shrug out of them. And then he was holding her bare breasts in his palms and whisking his thumbs over her taut nipples and her skin was turning goose-bumpy all over and it was like last night's adventure game in the hotel garden only much, much better.

'Jordan. Ooh-aah,' she managed, her breath hitching.

He was in total agreement and she knew there was no way he was going to allow anything or anyone to interrupt them this time. 'Swimsuit all-the-way off.'

He pushed his boxers down, but not before he produced a foil packet from somewhere and ripped it open with his teeth and sheathed himself beneath the water line while she peeled the Lycra down her thighs, then used her toes to push it the rest of the way. She tugged the band from her hair and ran her fingers through it, feeling like a goddess to his god.

They slid deeper into the cool blue depths together, eye to eye, skin to skin, foreheads touching, legs entwining, his erection hot and hard and heavy against her belly.

Not close enough. Not yet.

Water lapped at their shoulders, the palm fronds above them lazily limp in the heat that shimmered off the sand surrounding them. Nothing moved, nothing changed in this timeless spot, and for a moment it was as if the world were holding its breath, waiting.

Chloe knew *their* world wasn't waiting, the world of high finance and corporate luncheons to cater was far away, though in days this magical time would be over.

'This place is ours,' she said fiercely. 'This memory is ours.' And nothing could take that away from her. Gripping his jaw in her hands, she fused her mouth to his as if she could draw him into herself.

But he was the one who took control, took her under. Dark, dangerous delight as his tongue swept in to tangle with hers. Demand in his hands that seemed to be everywhere at once; her shoulders, her breasts, down her spine to cup her bottom and yank her closer.

Last night's starlit fantasy melted in the white-hot glare of a desert afternoon. There were no seductive word pictures this time, no whispered images and moonlight imaginings. Only moans and groans, need and greed.

Strong, relentless fingers found her centre. Fast slippery strokes, the glimpse of glory to come, and she gasped, her head falling back as the world spun out of control. Faster. Her entire body trembling now until the sky seemed to shimmer to white and explode into a million suns.

Before she could collapse, he caught her in the steel cradle of his arms and plunged inside her with a groan—one deep thrust to the hilt—driving her up again.

All she could see was him. In his eyes she saw blazing desire, demand and desperation. The words he muttered were hot and harsh and shockingly explicit against her mouth. She licked them from his tongue, then matched them with equal intensity, while her fingers kneaded and plucked and scraped whatever flesh they came in contact with.

Chloe raked unmerciful fingernails down his back, and Jordan gritted his teeth, pleasure balanced on a fine needle-point of pain. Her amber eyes shone—she knew exactly what she was doing.

The need for speed hammered through him, his blood echoing the same frantic rhythm, but he pulled out slowly, slowly, watching her eyes widen, her pupils dilate, a little panic filter through the haze. He smiled. *Payback.* Then plunged deep, back into that hot, tight paradise.

He'd known Chloe wasn't the submissive sort but he hadn't been sure if her adventurous spirit extended to her sexual preferences until now. Greed matched greed, heat matched heat, passion matched passion. Never had he found a woman so compatible with his own sexual desires. When he groaned she sighed. When he bowed, she arched. When he asked, she gave. She was a sensual whirlwind of perfume and water-slick skin. Peaches and cream and wild abandon.

She convulsed around him, her hands fisted against his chest, eyes glazed while she cried her triumphant release. His own vision blurred as he leapt over the sweet abyss with her.

CHAPTER ELEVEN

IT WAS A while before he could clear the haze from his mind and find his way back to something approaching rational. Somehow he'd managed to manoeuvre them both near enough to the edge of the pool to stretch out on the sand without drowning, and they lay wet and entwined like a couple of pieces of ragged river weed.

'We're going to burn,' she said lazily. 'All over. It won't be pretty. And it's guaranteed to be painful.'

He turned to look at her. Her arms were crossed over her eyes and her skin glistened with water but a satisfied smile curved her lips. In fact, she looked like the kitty cat who'd happily wallowed in a pond of cream.

His own smile was quick to follow. He rubbed the flat of his palm over the nearest breast and felt the hard little bead beneath. 'You'd be pretty whatever colour your skin was.'

She swiped at his arm. 'Charmer,' she said, not looking at him. 'Everyone knows lobster's *so* last century.' Shading her eyes, she sat up. 'I seem to have lost a swimsuit.'

'You don't need one. Skinny dipping's much more fun.' He caught the glint of his ring on her finger and something strange stole through him. Something almost possessive. He firmed his jaw. Whatever it was, it was dangerous. 'Time to move, then, if you don't want to burn.'

He gripped her wrists and pulled her up. Their naked bod-

ies bumped, those deep amber eyes met his. And again he
was flooded with a wave of unfamiliar emotion.

They'd had sex, that was all, he told himself. Good, fast,
honest, mind-blowing, mutually satisfying, all-the-way-to-
heaven-and-back sex. So what was this tender afterglow of
feelings? Why did he feel this…deep rush? Did she feel it
too? He remained still, cuffing her wrists, and staring into
her eyes searching for an answer. 'You okay?'

A fleeting shadow crossed her gaze but maybe he'd mis-
read it because it vanished with her smile. 'Besides needing
a shower and missing out on my spa session?' She planted a
kiss beneath his jaw. 'But I'm feeling entirely too ravished
to be annoyed. You?'

'We both know there was never a spa session and my back
will need some TLC later.'

'Ah…sorry about that…I'll make it up to you.'

She watched her finger tracing his left bicep and the in-
ferno he'd thought they'd doused for now sparked anew with
a speed and brightness that shocked him. More shocking; it
wasn't just spark that he wanted—he wanted *Chloe's* spark.
'I intend making sure you do. Chloe…'

'Yes?' Her finger remained where it was but her eyes
flicked to his again, alive and alluring.

*I want that feeling with you again. I want it so badly it
scares the hell out of me.* Her hand shifted slightly and the
ring drew his attention for a second time. Frowning, he
stepped back and brushed sand off his shoulders rather than
haul her closer and test how soon and how bright that spark
could catch again. 'Why don't you go have the first shower?'

'What, no showering with a friend?' Her voice was light
and teasing. 'This is the desert—we should all do our bit for
the planet.'

He walked to the table, picked up the bottles of cola now
wet with condensation and held one out to her. 'If we get into

that shower together, we're going to end up using a hell of a lot more water than our quota.'

She blushed, which was odd, he thought, considering she was unashamedly stark naked, and after what they'd just done to each other in broad daylight. She took the bottle from his fingers. 'Thanks.'

'I'll check out what's on the menu for dinner,' he said, deliberately turning away first.

Mindful of water conservation, Chloe showered fast with the fragrant gel provided. Her whole body sang—everywhere she touched she remembered how it had felt when Jordan had touched her. His magic fingers had wrought the most exquisite responses from her. No man had ever made her feel so alive. So feminine and desired.

She spent a longer time choosing from the scented massage creams on display and decided on a blend of frankincense, sandalwood, neroli and ylang ylang. The jar promised 'To instil peacefulness'. She figured she needed it. Because eventually somehow she'd have to pay the price for what she'd done.

She'd succumbed and made love with her business partner. Jordan Blackstone, millionaire bachelor and playboy. And she wasn't even sorry.

Yet.

She pushed negative thoughts away. Her reflection smiled back at her as she ran her fingers through her damp hair. Her shimmery off-one-shoulder kaftan with swirling colours of raspberry and tangerine highlighted the honey-blonde streaks. Her eyes looked bigger, brighter. I've-got-a-new-lover eyes. And with that warm glow to her skin, she actually looked pretty for once in her life.

You'd be pretty whatever colour your skin was.

Warmth closed around her heart like a gentle hand. Of course it was a line, and he'd been fondling her breast at the time, but it had made Chloe feel special. Sexy. Sensuous. Desired. And his eyes…she sighed…she was almost tempted to believe it hadn't been just about sex because for an instant she'd seen something deeper before he'd blinked it away. He'd asked her if she was okay then gallantly insisted she take her shower while he organised dinner.

He wasn't going to hang around when they got back to Australia—she wasn't his tall, glamorous brunette type with PhD and whatever else tacked on the end of her name. Their lives were worlds apart. But she'd discovered Jordan wasn't the shallow man she'd first thought. He was involved in charity work and genuinely cared about his staff and friends unlike so many men she'd met over the last few years. During this trip he'd been protective, considerate and generous.

She trusted him in a way she'd never trusted a man before. And against all the defences she'd put up, she was falling for him in a big way. It was so much more than just the business aspect of their relationship. He'd made her feel as if some dreams could come true. If nothing else, she was learning he was someone she could count on no matter what. He made her feel special.

She had a horrible fear there'd be tears when they parted. But hurts and disappointments and moving on were her life. She wouldn't change anything just because she was falling for a guy who wouldn't be there in the long term. She'd do what she always did—live for today and think about the future when it arrived.

While Chloe spent the next hour reading and relaxing in their luxury accommodation, Jordan showered then went over his plans for his meeting with the sheikh. She couldn't resist looking up every now and again to ensure it wasn't a dream. That the bare-chested man in the loose khaki shorts who'd done the wild thing with her was still there, and still as gorgeous and sexy as ever.

As the golden afternoon sky turned to crimson and purple and the air lost its sting, the Jeep arrived. The pair greeted their hosts and waited while Kadar and his wife unloaded fresh scented towels and trays of aromatic food.

Kadar raised flaps at intervals around the tent to let in the cooling breeze and bring the desert atmosphere inside while his wife spread the feast on a low table and lit fragrant sandalwood and beeswax candles inside the Moroccan lamps. The flickering light cast an intimate glow. They wished them a pleasant evening, then left discreetly.

'Hungry yet?' Jordan set his paperwork aside.

'Famished.' Chloe stretched luxuriously, then strolled to the table where Jordan was sitting and massaged his shoulders a moment. She loved that her new status as his lover gave her permission to touch him whenever she pleased. 'How about you?'

He grasped her hands over his shoulders, pulling her close and catching her ear between his teeth. 'So ravenous I could start on that delectable bare shoulder.'

'Later,' she promised. 'What have you ordered?'

'Come and find out.' He stood, and, fingers still linked, they walked to where the food was set.

He poured the chilled wine into what were probably genuine gold goblets, handed her one. 'To success.'

'To success.' Setting her goblet down, Chloe stabbed at a falafel with her fork, lifted it to her mouth and chewed. 'These are yummy.' She reached for another.

'Slowly. You'll give yourself indigestion.' He chuckled at her fast-food habit. 'This isn't Burger Supreme Central. Food is meant to be savoured and enjoyed. Try this.' He ladled something from a bowl, held the spoon out to her. 'Close your eyes and tell me what you can taste.'

'Turmeric, coriander, ginger and chilli. What is it?'

'Goat curry. One of my favourite dishes.'

The faint trickle of water and rustlings of tiny desert creatures beyond the tent could be heard between conversation that concentrated mainly on Jordan tutoring Chloe in the arts of leisurely fine wining and dining.

Eventually, Chloe excused herself to go to the bathroom. She almost laughed as she swished her hands beneath the tepid water. She'd served at fine dining functions rather than dined. But unlike Stewart, Jordan didn't seem to care about class distinctions; he treated people as equals.

She was drying her hands when she saw Jordan's wedding ring beside his toiletry bag and picked it up. Heavy. Must be worth a fortune. Why would he want to spend so much on a wedding ring for a fake marriage? As she held it in her palm she caught sight of some text inscribed inside. *Jordan and Lynette forever.* It was dated six years ago.

That lighter-than-air, on-top-of-the-world feeling deflated under the weight of doubts and questions.

Okay. Calm down, she told herself, her fingers curling around the ring. He wasn't married now.

Or was he?

Spots danced before her eyes. Had he been lying to her all along? Making a cheap and sordid mockery of what they'd done this afternoon?

No! She refused to believe it, but nevertheless a band clamped around her stomach, so tight she thought she might throw up.

Some things were none of her business but he hadn't simply left this information out of their conversation; he'd specifically told her he'd never been married.

By the time she went back inside, she had her nerves under control and joined him on the sofa where he'd poured Turkish coffee for both of them.

She took her cup and sipped. 'You're not wearing your ring.'

He glanced down at his bare finger. 'Noticed like a true wife.'

She fixed him with a stare. 'And you'd know this how? The wife bit,' she clarified, when his brows drew down in confusion. Or was it guilt?

'The suncream got under it when I rubbed you down. I took if off when I had a shower and forgot about it. It's in the bathroom…' His hesitation and his eyes told her what she wanted to know. 'You found it,' he said unnecessarily. Along with the information he'd neglected to mention.

'I did.' She held it up between finger and thumb, looked at the inscription again. 'Want to explain?'

'Not particularly.'

She wished her own expression were as skilled in keeping secrets as his was. 'I imagined you'd say that.' She set the ring on the table in front of him with a clink of metal on wood. 'Jordan and Lynette forever, huh?'

He tensed and a muscle in his jaw tightened. 'I'm not married, Chloe.' When she didn't answer—which in itself *was* her answer—he said, 'Don't you think the media would have had a field day with that information by now if Lynette and I had been married?'

She hadn't thought that far. 'You owe me some explanation at least.'

He raised his brows as if to say he owed her nothing of the kind. 'Do business partners need to know the intimate details of each other's love lives?'

He was coolly twisting this around to suit the circumstances. To suit himself. She reined in her resentment and the hurt. 'We went way past business partners this afternoon and you've made me feel like an idiot. You know about my family and why I agreed to this arrangement with you. I told you about Markos and how he made a fool of me.

'But you?' She pointed an accusing finger at his chest.

'You've kept yourself to yourself. And no one makes a fool of Jordan Blackstone, right? Because unlike some, you can afford to cover up a scandal.'

In the flickering light his expression changed, changed again. Acceptance to defensiveness to…understanding? 'Chloe. No scandal, I promise. And I'm sorry you feel that way. It wasn't my intention.'

'Not your intention to make a fool of me or not your intention to tell me about Lynette?'

Jordan saw a suspicious chin wobble and despised himself. His pride and his need for control—his *evasiveness*—had hurt the one person he least wanted to hurt. He reached out and cupped her jaw between his hands and looked into her eyes. 'Listen to me. You are *not* a fool, Chloe Montgomery. You're clever and honest and witty. You're generous and compassionate. And one of a kind.'

'High praise coming from my employer.' Her smile was tinged with sadness—as if those qualities he valued in her didn't count in her mind. As if she wanted more.

'Partner.' He hesitated. 'Friend.'

'Does the term *lover* scare you, Jordan?' She pushed his hands away from her face. 'But you're changing the subject. Again. If you don't want to talk about Lynette, that's *fine*.' She shrugged. 'It's not as if we're going to see each other after this week anyway.'

The words were unexpected and something flashed through his system and was gone, like lightning, leaving a strange burnt-out, hollow sensation. 'There's nothing in our agreement that says we can't continue to see each other if we want.'

Doubt and something like resignation clouded her eyes. '*If* we're in the same city. Or even in the same country.'

'Come here, Blondie.' He pulled her to him, tucked her against his side and kissed her sweet-smelling hair. Their relationship might be temporary but it wasn't over yet and he wanted to give her at least something of what she wanted to hear. 'Lynette was someone I met at uni.'

'Just *someone*? You had a wedding ring. Presumably she had one too. Oh…Jordan.' She turned her face up to his, a groove between her brows, her eyes worried. 'Please, don't tell me she…'

'No. We were going to get married. It just didn't happen.'

'Why not?'

'We wanted different things.'

'But you kept the ring,' she said softly. 'You wanted a re-minder.'

Hell, yes. 'Not for any foolish sentimental reason. I keep it to remind me that I'm not, and never will be, a marrying man.'

Her eyes welled up with sympathy. 'What did she do to destroy that for you?'

Frustrated that she'd assume a woman could wield that kind of power over him, he grabbed the damn thing, jammed it on his finger. 'What makes you think it was her? What makes you so sure I didn't break *her* heart?'

'I'm *not* sure. Because you haven't told me. But your words and actions since we agreed to this arrangement would in-dicate she's the one who did a number on you and not the other way round.'

The woman's insight and gentle compassion weren't some-thing Jordan knew how to deal with. She was scraping dan-gerously close to a raw spot he'd almost forgotten he had. 'It's in the past—leave it there.'

As a distraction, he touched her bare shoulder with a fin-ger—smooth ivory—and felt a little shiver run through her. 'We're never going to have another night like this, Blondie. Let's not waste it.'

Whisky eyes turned black in the amber candlelight and a

slow smile drifted over her lips. 'Let's not.' She rose and stood before him, gaze locked on his, confident in her femininity.

Sensing she wanted his attention for the moment but not his touch, he remained where he was. A messy flaxen halo around that elfin face with her too-big eyes that drew you in until you lost a part of yourself. Confident, yes, but also small and delicate and easily damaged. He wanted to tuck her inside the pocket of his jacket and keep her safe, next to his heart. *Just keep her...*

She pushed the garment off her shoulder and the silk slithered to the floor in a vibrant kaleidoscope of colour, leaving a vision of alabaster skin and lush curves and violet lace.

His heart pounded, his groin tightened and he curled his hands into fists on his thighs to stop himself reaching for her. Maybe it was the mystical romance of the silken tent or their exotic location or the drift of beeswax and sandalwood from the candles, but no woman had ever enchanted him so.

Was he ready for another woman in his life? he wondered. Then stopped wondering anything at all because all his blood drained from his brain as she unclasped her bra and dropped it at her feet. Her breasts were perfection, like succulent ripe fruit waiting to be relished.

She pushed the lace panties down over her hips and stepped out of them. A symphony of shadows and light played over her body. He might have groaned but he was no longer certain of his own responses, so absorbed was he with the vision in front of him.

Deep, intimate silence shimmered in the air between them, broken by the intermittent sputtering of a candle, a night creature fossicking in the palms outside, the sound of their own heightened breathing.

She held out her hands, candlelight gilding her eyes. 'Take me to bed, Jordan.'

He needed no second bidding. Scooping up her slender

form, he held her against his chest, and as he watched the emotion flicker over her face he lost himself for a moment in a fantasy.

She was as light as the desert breeze wafting through the hanging silks as he carried her to their bed. Because he just wanted to watch her a moment, he made a place for her amongst the mountain of pillows and laid her down. Stripping off his shorts, he climbed onto the bed, his thighs straddling hers.

To please himself, he fanned her hair out on either side of her head. To please her, he stroked her body from neck to thighs with feather-light touches that roused goose bumps along her flesh. To please them both, he lowered his mouth to one breast and closed his lips over the puckered tip while he brushed his fingers slowly over the curve of its twin.

They had all night so he lingered where he might have rushed. Took the time to enjoy the nuances of flavour and texture and fragrance—of her skin and hair, mouth and tongue. And she responded like a dream. Low intimate murmurs, the slow, sensuous glide of flesh on flesh, her hands and mouth unerringly seeking out places where he liked to be touched.

Rumpled silk sheets and air warm with the scent of passion. Candles sputtered and died. The velvet night seduced and soothed as the moon drifted across the sky, its cool light shafting through the tent's open flaps, painting skin an ethereal silver.

And when at last he lost himself inside her and the sounds of shared passion filled the air, it wasn't with a rush of speed, but with an abiding tenderness he'd never known he possessed.

CHAPTER TWELVE

CHLOE WOKE WITH the dawn—a rim of gold against the sand dunes and a chill in the dry air. She wanted to sigh and smile at the same time and hold the last few precious hours in her heart forever. Their magical Arabian night was over.

She didn't move lest she wake the man beside her. She wanted to look her fill of him first. Long black lashes swept down over his cheeks but that was where the innocent appearance stopped. A disreputable-looking night's growth dotted his square jaw; those lips, almost curving into a smile, were made for sin.

And she was tempted to sin some more. To taste, and touch and tease again. Tempted beyond all sane, logical reason.

Instead, she slid carefully out of bed, and, drawing a light shawl around her bare shoulders, she crept to the tent's flap and watched the harsh landscape welcome the day.

She needed to think where this thing with Jordan was going. Its speed and intensity scared her. *There's nothing that says we can't continue to see each other.* She remembered the expression in his eyes when he'd said those words. As if he meant it. The same look she'd seen when he'd made love to her in the moonlight.

I'm not a marrying man.

He confused her. She felt as if she were on a seesaw. He didn't want commitment—had made no secret of it. He wanted no-strings for as long as whatever it was they had lasted. Wasn't that what she wanted too? Free to walk away. No complications, no regrets, no tears.

I want to belong.

'What are you doing out of bed?' a sleep-husky voice said behind her.

And maybe it was his tone or something in the air between them because she imagined him saying that to her a year from now. Two. Twenty.

But she must keep it simple because he wouldn't be around; even a month was stretching it. Just sex, just for now. She dashed a suspicious moisture from her eye before she turned, her smile in place. 'Waiting for my lover to come find me.'

Warm hands drifted over her shoulders, then slipped beneath the shawl to stroke bare skin, but he'd seen her furtive action.

'He's here,' he murmured. 'And he wants to know who the low-life who hurt you is so he can go run him through with his sword.'

Her breath caught and she shook her head. She couldn't tell him how she really felt—how he would hate that. 'What are you talking about?'

'The scumbag who hurt you.' His voice tightened on the words. 'I asked you in the diner that first night we met. It's not Mr Despicable—he was never in your heart. There's someone else. Who was he, Blondie?'

Jordan's perceptiveness surprised her but the image that rose behind her eyes no longer harmed and humiliated. She was a stronger person than that naive young woman Stewart had used then tossed aside. More experienced. Wiser. It had taken Jordan to show her that.

'He doesn't matter. Not anymore.' Stewart was less than nothing. A faded scar. A lesson learned.

'You've never got him out of your system,' Jordan murmured against her neck. 'Now's a good time.'

He was right—the lying SOB needed to go. 'Rich English aristocrat. Widower. Huge country home. I was his son's nanny. Naive little Chloe fell in love and thought her love was returned. I was in such a hurry to tell my family the good news of my success and too stupid to realise that success didn't mean finding a rich man and falling in love.

'When he...' *threw me out* '...when I left, I didn't mention my failures to my family or that I'd moved on. Because we didn't keep in touch, they still think...' She shrugged.

'You are *not* a failure, Chloe.' He lifted her hair to kiss the back of her neck. 'You're a remarkable woman. You're gutsy and trustworthy. Someone others can count on.'

'Thank you.' He'd never know how much his words meant, more so because she knew they weren't empty platitudes. They lifted her up and made her want to sing. 'You can slay my dragons and demons for me any time.'

'Consider him slain.' His breath tickled the hairs at her temple. 'What would you have your lover do now?'

'I'd have him carry me back to bed and then...' She turned her head and whispered something in his ear that had that gorgeous mouth tilting up at the edges.

'My lady's wish is my command,' he said, and swung her up into his arms.

Twenty-four hours later they were preparing to meet the man Jordan hoped to forge a business deal with. The reason they'd come to Dubai. The reason she was here, Chloe reminded herself, checking her appearance in the mirror.

Satisfied she looked the part of wife with her conservative navy blue business suit and demure cream blouse and her hair swept back into a neat chignon by the hotel's stylist, she exited the bathroom in search of Jordan.

They'd returned to the city late yesterday. Their honey-moon night was a beautiful memory but, if last night was an indication, the rest of their time in Dubai promised to be almost as memorable.

She saw him standing by one of the panoramic windows overlooking the beach scrolling through emails on his phone, brows drawn in concentration. His made-to-measure suit accentuated his broad shoulders and long legs and his shirt looked whiter-than-white against his tanned skin. A navy tie completed the corporate image.

But now she knew the body beneath the clothes. The man behind the image. She knew what he liked, what made him come. Who he was when he wasn't being Jordan Blackstone, gold-mining magnate.

She admired that man. She respected him. He'd given her a new belief in herself and lifted her self-esteem. He'd shown her that not all men were bastards.

Almost reluctant, she stepped farther into the room and announced her presence. 'When do we leave?'

'In a few moments.' He looked up and smiled, checking out her appearance with a nod of approval. 'Perfect. I swear I've never met a more punctual woman. Punctual *and* beautiful.'

'That's why you married me, right, Pookie?'

His smile dipped a moment like the sun skimming behind a solitary cloud in a blue sky. 'Very good, Blondie. Keep it up and it's going to work to both our advantage. Only a few more hours and if everything goes to plan…'

They'd be going home. She crossed the space between them and straightened his tie even though it didn't need straightening—everything about Jordan was precise. Understated and refined. His aftershave was cool and subtle. 'You'll wow him with that fantastic business plan of yours and with your commitment and morals. He'd be an idiot to refuse you over that other Xmining company.'

'X23.' He tipped her chin up and looked into her eyes. 'Thanks for your confidence in me—it means a lot. And thanks for doing this entire thing on such short notice.'

'You paid me to do a job.' Hardly aware she was doing it, she twisted the ring on her finger.

He nodded. 'So it's the beauty session at last, then. Or is it a spa?'

'Spa and massage. I can't wait. You see, I have these tight muscles...'

Jordan chuckled, and she smiled back at him, sharing the humour and fun. She'd been expecting to spend the day with Qasim's wife and other female members of his family but the elderly woman was still by her sister's bedside since she'd suffered a severe heart attack. It had been decided that Chloe would meet the sheikh, then be free to choose her own activities for the day.

'One more thing before we leave.' Jordan pulled a slim box from his jacket pocket and opened it. 'This is for you.'

She stared at the slim gold chain and a pair of gold filigree hoop earrings nestled in royal blue velvet. Was this a thank-you gift or a lover's gift? Or investment pieces to wear for the day? She didn't ask. Not now.

'I bought it from one of Qasim's shops the other day,' Jordan explained and lifted the chain from its box. 'He'd expect the owner of a successful gold mine to shower his new wife with gold. Chosen specifically for her, even if she's not into jewellery. Turn around.' He fastened it around her neck. 'I'll let you do the earrings.'

'I need a mirror.' Distracted, she withdrew her compact and removed the tiny sleepers she'd worn for years then slid the golden hoops in. Maybe it was the residual passion from the past couple of days but she looked different wearing Jordan's jewellery. And he'd chosen it for her.

'Sophisticated and classy,' he said.

'They're not words I associate with myself,' she replied, still studying herself critically.

'Well, you should start associating them, because they suit you—the words and the jewellery.'

Sophisticated? Chloe Montgomery? He meant it but with every second that ticked by she felt less like herself and more like a woman she'd never met and didn't know.

Or maybe he'd brought out the real Chloe, the one she could be if given a chance. She spun away towards the elevator, tossing her compact in her purse. 'You do *not* want to be late. I'm making sure you're not.'

'Aren't you going to give me a kiss for luck?'

'You don't need luck—you already have enough of everything else to make this work.'

Their meeting was scheduled in one of the hotel's private meeting rooms. They were received by one of Sheikh Qasim's advisers and ushered into a luxurious blue room large enough to hold fifty people. The man promptly disappeared, leaving them in a kind of limbo. Which Jordan seemed to expect.

Not to worry—smiling waiters served them spiced tea and a variety of delicacies while they waited. And waited. And waited. If Jordan was nervous, he didn't show it. He assured Chloe waiting was the norm here.

A long, fraught hour or more later, the door opened and the elderly man walked in, his robes swirling about him.

Jordan and Chloe both stood. Jordan stepped forward, extending his hand. 'Sheikh Qasim bin Omar Al-Zeid. *Salam alaykum.*' Peace be upon you.

The sheikh met Jordan and clasped his hand firmly. *'Wa alaykum as-salam.'*

'Sheikh Qasim bin Omar Al-Zeid, I'd like to introduce my wife.' He placed a light hand on her back and smiled into her eyes. 'This is Chloe Montgomery.'

The sheikh turned to Chloe, nodded respectfully. *'Salam alaykum.'*

'Wa alaykum as-salam.' Smiling, Chloe inclined her head.

A short time later, the introductions over, pleasantries exchanged and sincere thanks given for the 'honeymoon special', Chloe was finally able to escape to her massage appointment. Gratefully. *Very* gratefully. Tricky etiquette in this part of the world. For Jordan's sake, she hoped she'd got it right. He'd paid for her services and she'd smiled and acted the docile, adoring wife and just prayed it had worked. If it was successful, they were booked on tomorrow's flight. Which meant tonight was their last night.

Her heart was already bleeding. So she did what any woman would do under the circumstances—she distracted herself. If she didn't do *something*, she'd end up pacing a bald track in their suite's very expensive carpet. And she needed, desperately, to maintain some control over her circumstances.

Hours later Chloe received a call. 'Break out the champagne,' Jordan told her with a grin a mile wide in his voice. 'I'm on my way up to the room.'

And she could visualise that familiar spark in his eyes, the way his cheeks creased when he smiled, and wished she could be there right now to plant one on him. 'Jordan, that's wonderful news, congratulations. I'm so happy for you, but I'm not there.'

Jordan frowned as he stepped into the elevator, his effervescent mood losing some of its fizz. What did she mean, she wasn't there? Surely a massage didn't last that long? 'It's gone three—where are you?'

'I'm in the Burjuman Centre making the most of what's left of my time here.'

'Shopping.' A ridiculous feeling of disappointment rolled through him. He stared unseeing at the world falling away as the elevator soared skywards. She was shopping while he'd been making one of the most important deals of his life.

'I'm sorry,' he heard her say. 'I lost track of time. I'm leaving right this minute. Don't start without me, okay?'

'Okay.' He disconnected, stepped out into their suite muttering to himself. Her stories must be having an effect on him because for some insane reason he'd expected her to be waiting with bated breath for his triumphant return, the way a lady waited in the castle for her battle-weary hero.

Blimey, what an idiot.

When it came right down to it, why would it matter to Chloe how his meeting went? She'd done her bit. For her this whole business was over. She could walk away now, well recompensed for her time and trouble, and never have to see him again.

The question was, would she?

The more disturbing question was would he let her?

He ordered the most expensive bubbly on the menu then strode to the windows and watched the afternoon sun shimmering on the gulf. Forty-eight hours ago they'd been making love in a desert oasis under that afternoon sun. Now... He dismissed the wet and wild images. *Priorities, man.* He'd secured a buyer for his gold as he'd promised his father; that was what was important here.

But when she rushed across the room towards him thirty minutes later, pink-cheeked and pretty in a new fuchsia sundress with a matching bolero, her eyes sparkling with excitement—for *his* success—he wondered for a few mad seconds whether his long-held, sharply focused priorities had blurred.

'Congratulations!' She didn't give him time to clear that haze, dropping her bag and launching herself at him with an enthusiastic 'You did it!' and smacking her lips to his.

When she might have pulled away he clamped his hands to her head—he wasn't settling for anything that brief. Prying her lips apart with his tongue, he swirled inside and turned a simple kiss into something deeper and a lot more complicated. She yielded without surrendering, her familiar taste spinning through his senses like a favourite whisky.

'Not without your help,' he murmured when they finally broke apart, gasping and staring at each other as if they were looking at strangers. As if something had changed.

Everything had changed. It was time to go home. And they both knew it.

'We made a good team today,' she said, quickly busying herself kneading his shoulders with her thumbs and nipping at his jaw with her teeth.

He walked his fingers all the way down her spine and tucked her close so she fitted against him, snug as moss on a log. 'We're good together.'

'Yes…'

Rucking up her skirt then winding her arms around his neck, she practically climbed up him and hooked her legs around his waist. Her feminine heat pressed against his pelvis, her intoxicating eyes…he could drown in those eyes… If he wasn't careful. If he was honest…

'There's something I want to tell you first,' he said, holding her close. 'I came clean with Qasim. I told him we weren't married.'

She leaned back to look at him, her hands still around his neck. 'After all the trouble and expense you went to? Why?'

'It just seemed wrong. It *was* wrong. I've wanted this for so long. Winning this meant so much to me that I lost sight of everything else. But I realised today when I walked into that room that I wanted to win it without resorting to deception.'

She nodded. 'I'm glad. It's much better this way.'

He saw the questions in her eyes and he suddenly wanted to share his story with her. 'I want to I tell you why this is so important to me.'

'Okay,' she said quietly, and slid down his torso until her feet touched the ground.

Without letting her go, he led her to a window seat and sat her down and looked into those liquid amber eyes. 'You already know my father died before he could close an important deal he'd set up in the UAE. But what I didn't tell you was that I was a selfish, self-centred undergraduate who was flunking his course and should have been there for him when he needed me...'

When he was done telling her, she squeezed his hand, her eyes filled with understanding and respect. 'You'd have made him so proud today.'

'I promised him I'd fix it if it was the last thing I did and I think I managed that.' He felt lighter, as if a huge weight had been lifted. Finally, after all the years of hard work, he'd found some sort of closure. And sharing the moment with Chloe was something he'd always remember.

'So, what did Qasim say when you told him about us?' Chloe asked.

'That he appreciated my honesty. He told me I was the best man for the job whether I was married or not.'

She nodded. 'You didn't need me after all.'

He shook away a sudden melancholy her words invoked and dragged her onto his lap, spreading her thighs on either side of his. 'It was much more fun with you along.'

'It has been fun.' She seemed as keen as him to change the mood. 'And I've made plans. Tonight's on me. And you too, if you like.' She grinned and he caught her meaning.

'I like.' Grinning back, he spread his hands beneath her buttocks, fingers skimming the edge of her panties. 'Very much. But I thought you liked being on top?'

'I like being any which way with you. But about dinner— why don't we go back to our little beach-side place? This is our Last Supper—I'd like to end where we began. Closure and all that.'

'We don't have to leave tomorrow,' he decided. He'd change their flights. 'We could take a couple more days…' He wasn't ready to go home to his all-work no-play world yet. They weren't done. In fact, they'd only just started.

Her agile body stilled. 'And then what?'

'Try skiing Dubai style and sleeping in till noon with not much sleeping going on…' He trailed off because the eyes staring into his weren't the let's-have-fun ones he'd just been looking at.

'It's not going to change anything, Jordan.'

What wasn't? 'Not sure what you mean.'

'It's only delaying the inevitable. We agreed to do this. And now it's done. Over.'

Jordan stared at her, a not-so-good feeling in his gut. 'What are you saying?'

'I don't want us to linger on and die a slow, painful death. And that's what's going to happen with us. We might have a fantastic meal tonight and follow it up with equally fantastic sex—*Pookie*—but if we let it continue eventually it's going to fade because that's all we have in common. And that's not taking into consideration your busy schedule and my propensity for not sticking around.'

'Yeah, but until then—'

'So when we get home—'

'That's it.'

She nodded, her eyes not quite meeting his. 'I told you, I finish what I start. No loose ends before I move on.'

Or did she leave before someone else finished whatever it was for her?

'Chloe…' He trailed off because what could he say? She had it right. No loose ends. They'd had fun and they'd always known it was only about the business deal with a little diversionary side-trip along the way. She didn't want to live in his world, nor had he asked her to. Sometimes he didn't want to live in it either. There were days he wished he could chuck the whole thing in and be like Chloe—free as the wind, no employees depending on him for an income. An unknown face in the crowd.

If she wanted to leave tomorrow, so be it. 'We'd better make the most of the rest of the time we have left, then.'

She leaned in so that every luscious part of her touched every wire-taut part of him, then reached for his belt buckle. 'That's what I was hoping you'd say...'

Chloe was determined to make the evening special—a time to remember. She'd arranged the table with the best view over the beach, best French champagne to toast their success. She recounted her adventures and challenged Jordan to pick the fake—the near disastrous white-water rafting expedition, her night in a haunted castle with a team of paranormal investigators, the evening she and a girlfriend had ended up in a well-known movie star's suite sipping bubbly with the cast of her latest blockbuster.

He listened to her as if what she had to say was worth something. Not only listened, but actually conversed with her on topics they'd never covered. He seemed to understand her on so many levels and, for the first time in what seemed like forever, she felt uplifted, valued, appreciated.

After dinner they strolled along the beach talking of anything and everything, then sat on the sand, stared up at the northern constellations and shared the evening's silence. Their fingers were barely touching yet it was as if he'd become an integral part of who she was. Warming her body, unlocking her heart and breathing life into her soul.

She couldn't allow herself to fall further and yet she feared it was already too late.

* * *

Later, in their suite with the moonlight casting bars across the floor, he took his time removing her clothes, lingering over every centimetre of skin he bared as if each were a rare jewel. When she was naked, he knelt before her and worshipped her body with a skill and expertise she could only shiver and sigh and moan over.

And when she could no longer stand, he laid her on the bed and continued his homage to her womanhood with hands and mouth, teeth and tongue. Time drifted like the gentle lap and wash of the tide and she clung to him to keep from floating away. Who knew a man's touch could be so slow and easy? Or his body so finely crafted that he was masculine perfection?

He slid his perfect body on top of her then—hard muscle and warm skin a spine-tingling friction. She drew a luxurious breath, inhaling his personal scent and the faint fragrance of Eastern spices. Then forgot to breathe at all as she looked into his midnight-blue eyes and flew with him over the edge of their magic carpet fantasy.

I love you.

Simple.

Impossible.

Finally, energy spent and desire sated, tangled together on the silken sheets, they slept.

CHAPTER THIRTEEN

THEY LANDED IN Melbourne late at night during a rainstorm. The heavy sky was still spitting its vengeance on the windscreen as Jordan's chauffeured car neared the CBD. Which was only fitting, Chloe thought. She'd wear the weather as an accessory. That way no one would notice her mood or her tears. Except she was determined not to cry until she reached the privacy of her bedroom.

She'd planned to get her own cab but there was no press around and cabs were thin on the ground, so Jordan's car it was. They'd barely spoken during the flight, made easier by their individual wraparound seats. Thank God for wealthy businessmen. Both of them had been tired after almost no sleep the previous night, so, apart from when Jordan had been working furiously on his laptop or on the phone, most of the time one or the other had been asleep.

Or in Chloe's case, pretending to be. It had been hard, but necessary, and it had left her almost dead on her feet, a blessing, she hoped, that would help her crash out for the next twelve hours.

The car turned into her street. 'It's late,' he said. 'Stay at my apartment tonight.'

Her heart leapt at his invitation, but she pressed her lips together and looked out of the window. It was only delaying the inevitable and she didn't want to see his apartment. To know where he lived and imagine him there. Worse, imagine him there with another woman. 'No, Jordan.'

'Then let me stay here. With you.'

Something in his tone had her turning to him. She'd never seen that look in Jordan's eyes. Clearly, he wasn't used to being turned down. 'I told you my bed's too small.'

He looked as if he might argue, then glanced at the driver up front, and Chloe realised it was costing Jordan to sweet-talk her into something he must know she'd refuse in front of his staff.

'I have a headache,' she improvised for the sake of his pride as they pulled into the kerb. 'Jet lag. I need an uninter-rupted night's sleep.'

The driver climbed out to retrieve her luggage from the boot, leaving them alone in the back seat. She dug through her bag ostensibly looking for her keys.

'So this is it, then.' His voice was hard and remote-sounding.

'Yes.' She heard the tremor in her voice and tightened her fingers around her keys, then hoisted her bag onto her shoul-der, desperate to get away. 'Thanks for—'

'Save it.' He wrenched his door open. 'Like it or not, I'm walking you to your damn door. You can *thank* me then.'

Rain spat on her face, chilling her as she hurried up the path, Jordan following with her bag. Somehow she got the key in the lock, then turned to him. Thankfully the security light didn't seem to be working and it was dark under the veranda. But not dark enough to miss the granite set of his jaw, the flash of—was that temper?—in his eyes.

Why? Because he hadn't got his own way? Something inside her responded in kind. And far better for her self-preservation to turn her misery into irritation or annoyance. Just because she'd gone and fallen in love with him didn't mean she was going to let him change her mind and go against what she knew was the right decision. For both of them.

So toughen up, Chloe. She wasn't going to apologise for her choice. He had a masters degree in seduction and another in persuasion and she wasn't going to allow a man to make her decisions for her ever again.

'Chloe. Listen up.' Stepping close, he tilted her face up to his with a finger so she had no choice but to look into his eyes, shuttered now, betraying little of what he was feeling. His temper seemed to have dissipated and he spoke with a measured calm. 'I don't want to stop seeing you but I made a promise when we signed our agreement. I'm not going to force you into something you don't want.'

'Tha—'

'Or should I say, what you *do* want but you're too afraid to admit.' His hand fell away and he stepped back, leaving her feeling chilled to the bone and totally exposed because he read her like a book.

She firmed her chin. 'With regards to our *business* arrangement, if anything changes with Qasim or the deal, and you need my assistance, please let me know.' She knew she sounded PA prim.

His eyes held hers captive. 'If you change your mind about *us*, or decide to come clean with me, you have my contact details.'

He didn't kiss her goodbye, just spun on his Italian leather shoe's heel and walked down her path, his black cashmere coat flapping behind him. Taking her heart with him.

But not her independence, not her identity. She still had those, at least. *And will they keep you warm on a cold winter's night?* a little voice whispered.

At the gate he turned back, spine rigid, his eyes darker than midnight. 'You say you like to finish what you start. We started something and it's not finished, so I'm wondering, how do those loose ends sit with you, Chloe?'

Then he was gone.

Three days later, from his expansive view in one of Perth's newest office buildings, Jordan rolled his executive chair back and watched the western sky grow pink behind a bank of mushroom-coloured clouds. It was the first time he'd taken a break since he'd started work at five a.m.

He'd sent his PA away and told her he wasn't to be disturbed under any circumstances. Roma had asked did that include coffee? before his frown had answered for him and he hadn't seen a glimpse or heard a peep from her since.

A knock sounded at his door and an unsmiling Roma poked her head in. She was an attractive forty-something brunette and Jordan valued her highly. 'I'm leaving now,' she said, and held a small packet out for him. 'This came this afternoon, registered express post. Thought it might be important and I didn't want to just leave it…'

Hell. Her tone and body language made him feel as if he'd kicked a puppy. 'Thanks, Roma.' When she didn't come any closer, he crossed the room and took it from her. 'Bad day.' He forced a smile. 'Guess I won't win employer of the year.'

'Maybe not this year.' A tentative smile crossed her face. 'I know this trip's been stressful…' She hesitated, as if waiting for an explanation. When none was forthcoming, she went on, 'I'll be going, then, if there's nothing further you need. Or if you want to talk…' She shook her head once. 'Guess not.'

'I'm fine, Roma. Thanks. See you tomorrow.' If she hadn't tendered her resignation, that was. Ah… 'Roma?'

She turned, warily. 'Yes?'

'How's Bernie?' Roma's husband was also an employee, a geologist up north in one of his mines.

Her brows lifted, puzzled. 'Fine, last we spoke. He's due home in a fortnight.'

Jordan nodded. 'I find myself in the rather desperate position of being dateless for the Rapper One ball and—'

'You want me to find you a *date*?' Her eyes widened and her voice rose a notch.

'No, no. Not that. I know you and Bernie attended last year so I was wondering—rather, *hoping*, since Bernie can't be here with you this year—that you'd accompany me instead.'

'Oh.' A long awkward pause. 'Well. That sounds…nice.'

'I'll ring Bernie myself and check with him first to make sure he's okay with it. I promise to work on my social skills in the meantime.'

Her smile warmed a few degrees and the Roma he knew shone through. 'You do that and I'll talk Bernie into letting me buy a new outfit.'

'Great. Have a good evening. And I'll put the word on Bernie about that new dress.'

He watched her leave, then turned the mystery packet over in his hands and read the sender's address. *Chloe Montgomery*. His gut cramped and he traced her scrawled handwriting as if he could bring her to him by touch. Images of her shot back. Hair that reminded him of sunlight. Her smile that could light up his day—and his night. The last time he'd seen her, on her veranda and telling him it was over.

She hadn't been smiling then.

He ripped through the packaging and withdrew a familiar box. 'Dammit, Blondie,' he muttered, already knowing what he'd find—the gold jewellery and the wedding ring.

And what the hell was he supposed to do with them? He ran his fingers along the slim gold chain, remembering how she'd looked that morning he'd clasped it around her neck. Understated elegance. The kind of woman who'd make any man proud to have her by his side, be it business or pleasure.

He'd never forget the way she'd supported him that day, her enthusiasm when he'd told her he'd won the old sheikh over.

And now she'd tossed his gift back in his face. By remote. Did she care so little about him that she wanted no reminders at all? Had what they'd shared meant nothing? Had she just been waiting for that second payment to go into her account—which he'd attended to first thing this morning—and now further contact was unnecessary? Unwanted?

His fingers tightened on the chain momentarily before he slipped it back in its box, flipped the lid shut and shoved it back in its post pack.

No loose ends.

Her words echoed in his head and he refused to acknowledge the way his whole body tensed and constricted as his control over his emotions slipped a notch. He'd all but begged her to let him stay the night. He stalked grimly across the room. He never allowed emotion to gain the upper hand. Why waste time thinking about a woman who was probably already on her way out of the country?

On an oath, he shoved the packet in his wall safe, slammed the door shut, effectively putting a full stop at the end their relationship. *Done.* She had her clean break as she wanted.

And wasn't that what he wanted too?

'So you're serious about leaving Melbourne?'

Dana's voice penetrated Chloe's thoughts and she realised she wasn't in a silken tent in Dubai, she was in a commercial kitchen prepping for tomorrow morning's breakfast function and had no idea what her boss had just said. She blinked away the daydream. 'Pardon?'

'Are you sure about moving on? You just started here and you said you like it.'

'I'm sorry, circumstances have made it necessary for me

to move on.' The possibility of running into Jordan was just too likely here working with Dana.

'By "circumstances", you mean Jordan.'

Chloe was slicing glacé cherries and her knife slipped. *'Ouch.'*

'You okay?'

Chloe checked that no skin was broken and continued. 'Yep.'

'Can you check the inventory on my PC for me?' Dana slid the last tray of cheese platters into the fridge and indicated her PC tablet on the nearby desk with her chin. 'I want to make sure we didn't forget to add those canapés tomorrow night's client ordered at the last minute. And watch your fingers. I don't want blood in my fruit compotes.'

'Watching,' Chloe murmured, and set her knife down, wiped her hands and crossed the room. At her touch the screen lit up and she found herself staring at a society news page.

Jordan.

For an instant her heart soared like a bird. then dived to her feet as if she'd been shot. Jordan, looking sexy as sin in his tux and escorting an attractive brunette to some charity event in Perth two nights ago. *His* charity. He'd never mentioned the function to Chloe.

Ridiculous to be jealous. She refused to think about the fact that it had been nearly two weeks since she'd told him it was over—obviously he'd wasted no time moving on to the next available woman.

No thanks to Dana for interfering.

She slapped the cover over the screen, and met her boss's eyes. 'Not fair, Dana.' Her lips felt numb, her legs felt like water. Untying her apron, she headed for the door.

'Chloe, it's his PA. Roma West. And she's very married.'

'So?' She stopped, told her trembling self it didn't matter. 'What's your point?'

'You're in love with him. I wanted to be sure. And I do know what you were doing in Dubai.'

Not everything, Chloe hoped. She crushed the corners of her apron between her fingers and forced herself to walk back to her station. Calm, steady. 'You're way over the line. And you're wrong. Why would I want to fall in love with an arrogant, domineering man like your friend Jordan Blackstone?'

'Wanting has nothing to do with it. And do *not* pick up that knife.' Swooping in, Dana finished slicing the last few cherries, popped them on the top of the little glass bowls then carried the tray to the fridge. 'If he meant nothing to you, you wouldn't have reacted that way.'

That jealous, vulnerable way. Chloe swiped up a cloth and began wiping down surfaces. 'So what if I am?' Then she sucked in a breath because suddenly her secret was out and she hadn't ever meant for it to be.

'It's okay,' Dana said quietly. 'I won't say anything.'

'Is it that obvious?' God, no, please not.

'The look on your face just then? And you came back to work even though Jordan had paid me enough to cover your wages for the next week. Believe me, *that's* not normal behaviour.'

'I like to work,' Chloe told her. 'It's therapeutic.'

No matter how healthy her bank balance was— 'Does *he* know? Did he say something?'

'Not to me he hasn't. And if he knows, would that be so bad?'

'Absolutely.' Oh, she'd be mortified. Her one-sided love was tragedy enough without letting the hapless victim in on it. A man who saw women as manipulative and money-hungry.

'Why?'

She feigned indifference and rinsed out her cloth. 'A man's too complicated. I'm not in one place long enough…'

'Sometimes you need to stop a while and listen to your heart.'

'I… Maybe.' And suddenly something inside her yearned for a piece of that slow-down time. Time to make a home of her own where she could paint the walls whatever colour she wanted. Where she could plant bulbs and watch them flower for more than one springtime.

Not some palatial English manor she'd never belong in, but her own place.

A place to put down roots like those spring bulbs.

And she could do that now, she realised. Ironic that it was Jordan who'd made it possible when he wasn't going to be a part of it. Her heart plunged down the sinkhole with the water. She knew enough about him to know she loved him, but not enough, perhaps, to fully understand him. 'That function he was at…his charity, isn't it? It obviously means a great deal to him.'

'Yes.'

'Why is he so devoted to helping troubled teens?'

'It stems from his past. He had a tough childhood that no kid should have to grow up with.'

'I know he loved his dad, so was it his mother? He refused to speak about her.'

'He won't speak about her to anyone, but, according to Sadiq, she was a witch and his father was too weak to stand up to her.'

'Poor kid.' She understood rejection, and her heart twisted for what Jordan the child must have endured that he refused to acknowledge his own mother and counselled troubled youth.

'Whatever you do, don't let him hear your sympathy.' Dana cleaned the knife and put it away. 'Let's call it a night here.'

'But I haven't fin—'

'The morning's soon enough.' Dana glanced at her watch, answered an incoming text before slipping her phone in her bag and marching Chloe to the door by her elbow. 'Come on, we're going to unwind with a cappuccino at my favourite Chapel Street café. My treat, and I'm not taking no for an answer.'

Chloe frowned down at her flat shoes, work trousers and 'Dana's Events' monogrammed uniform top. Unlike Dana, who hadn't been wearing a uniform and had managed to grab her high-fashion fur coat on the way out.

'I'm hardly dressed for going out. Are you sure you don't need to be somewhere?'

'Only somewhere warm and cosy and familiar where the coffee's hot and the lights are low.'

'So you and Chloe enjoyed your *honeymoon*.' Sadiq leaned back in the dimly lit, high-backed booth specifically chosen for its privacy in the back of a classy out-of-the-way upstairs café on Chapel Street and studied Jordan over the rim of his glass. 'Qasim mentioned it.'

'Of course he did.' Jordan tipped back his glass, swallowed long and deep. 'Did he tell you the rest?'

'He admired your honesty and courage and thought Chloe would be a good partner for you when you decide to make it legitimate. He's not as unyielding as we thought.'

Jordan didn't answer. *In a magic kingdom far, far away lived a princess with flaxen hair and amber eyes.* Storybook stuff.

'Is she the reason you're back in Melbourne again so soon?'

Sadiq's question interrupted Jordan's thoughts and he blinked away the image. 'Had some work on the Tilson mine.'

'Right.'

'Yeah.' *Have you seen her?*

'No. But I reckon you need to.'

Crikeys, had he spoken aloud? 'You're starting to sound like your wife.'

'Just saying. No reason to get defensive. Or is there?' he murmured. 'You never said how you two got on.'

Jordan took a while to answer. This was Sadiq, his best mate. The one who'd been there when Lynette had disappeared. 'She was different. She wasn't like any woman I've ever met—she saw me…differently.'

'And it scares the hell out of you. Is that why you've relegated her to the past tense?'

'Fact is, she didn't want to continue what we had—how did she put it? No loose ends. So it's a moot point.'

'And you didn't try to convince her otherwise?'

'Why would I? One thing I'll say for Chloe, she's got a sensible head on her shoulders.' Those beautiful creamy elegant shoulders…

'What if she walked in here now?'

'What if she did?' He shrugged, unwilling to contemplate that scenario because there were too many unresolved questions.

'What if she told you she'd changed her mind?'

'Maybe I'd tell her I'd changed mine now.' His fists tightened on the tabletop. 'I won't be manipulated by a woman's passing whims.'

'No one's manipulating you, mate. Chloe's not Lynette.'

'There you are.' At the sound of Dana's voice, Jordan looked up and was confronted by not one manipulative woman, but two.

And then I saw her face… As he stared at the woman he hadn't seen in twelve days, give or take a couple of hours, the words from a familiar pop song danced through his head, carving up a path straight to his heart where they continued to stomp and stamp like a wild rock concert.

He heard Chloe's stifled gasp and even though the lights

were dim her eyes looked like saucers, her complexion as pale and fragile as eggshell. She looked a hell of a lot like he felt. She was also wearing one of those unflattering Dana's Events uniforms so maybe she was as innocent in this set-up as he.

Sadiq slid out of the high-backed bench seat and rose. 'Dana and I are off to check out the latest sci-fi movie. Catch you two later.'

'Hang on—'

'No—'

Both he and Chloe protested at the same time.

Jordan stood, their partners in crime left and the two of them stared at each other.

'I know you think I had something to do with this,' Chloe said before he could speak, her eyes willing him to believe her. 'But I didn't.'

'Seems fate threw us together one more time.'

'Not fate, just two meddling friends of yours.'

'They'll keep. Might as well have a seat now you're here.'

She hesitated before sliding into the seat opposite. 'I won't stay long, I've got an early start tomorrow.'

'Don't we all? Coffee?'

'Thank you.'

He summoned the waiter hovering nearby and ordered two cappuccinos. 'You caught up with your parents yet?'

'Only by email but they're very grateful for the money. So thanks. I told them about…the breakup with Stewart and leaving—thanks to you for that too because I needed a kick up the backside to make it happen.'

'That's good to hear.'

'Mum actually asked when I'm coming home. She's finally emailing me herself now.'

'She misses you. They all miss you.'

'Maybe. I never thought they did.'

'Maybe you never gave them a chance.'

'Maybe I was afraid to.'

'You're going to tell them everything then?'

'Not everything.' He heard the hint of humour in her voice.

'I've missed you too, Chloe.' The words slipped from his mouth before he could call them back.

'Oh.' Her whole being seemed to light up like the sun appearing after morning mist and her eyes splashed with warmth and for a crazy second he thought maybe she'd missed him too, but then that grey mist rolled back and her smile wasn't the smile he wanted to see. It was brittle and way too bright when she said, 'Bet you say that to all the girls.'

Dammit, Chloe. He'd thought he'd conquered vulnerability years ago but the iron fist squeezing his chest disabused him of that notion. That old feeling of craving even a scrap of his mother's affection slid back like a dark tide. A kid's lack of understanding. The hurt of being ignored. Resented.

'Knowing my reputation with women, wouldn't those sentiments be counter-productive?' He pasted some kind of a grin on his lips that felt as if it didn't belong. 'After all, I wouldn't want them getting the wrong idea, would I?'

Chloe's expression froze and she didn't answer, sliding the sugar bowl around on the table between them in quick little circles and changing the topic. 'I read your charity ball was a success. Not that I was checking up on you,' she added quickly. 'Dana *happened* to arrange for me to see a picture of you and your PA posing for the cameras.'

'Did she?' he clipped.

'You're big news in W.A. Australia-wide, in fact.' She waved a hand about them, reminding him again of the way she moved—with elegance and a charming carelessness that had fascinated him from day one. 'No wonder this place is so hard to get into and dimly lit and private for the right people. You really are a celebrity.' Her eyes were dark honey tonight and everywhere but on his.

'I'm as ordinary as you.' Reaching over the table, he
wrapped a hand around her busy one, waiting until he had
her full attention to say, 'I know a place not far from here
that's much more private.'

CHAPTER FOURTEEN

'MY CAR'S PARKED not far up the street. Are you game?' he asked when she didn't say anything.

Chloe was too stunned to answer. His voice was like velvet and addictive. She'd missed hearing that voice. The only time she heard it lately was in her sleep; when she managed to get to sleep, that was. She knew it was a bad decision, but always-up-for-a-challenge Chloe allowed her hand to be swallowed up in Jordan's, and her head nodded almost without her consent.

She saw his eyes darken to midnight-blue as they slid out of the booth together. She followed him through the dimly lit café, down the narrow stairs and outside where the air was fresh and the bump of nearby music throbbed up through the pavement.

He didn't ask what transport she'd used, escorting her protectively past a throng of party-goers. She breathed in his scent, the warmth of his hand at her back familiar and as comforting as it was arousing.

They passed a trendy clothing store, its light spilling over them, neon and bright. Every second stretched, every step seemed to take forever. Her breaths became shorter, shallower as urgency twisted like a live wire inside her and she realised they were almost running.

That might have been the reason they almost crashed into

a middle-aged couple coming from the opposite direction, but the instant they greeted Jordan by name Chloe knew they recognised him and had stepped into their path deliberately.

'Well, if it isn't Jordan Blackstone.'

'Evening, Jordan.' The couple spoke at the same time. The woman dripped with jewellery of the genuine kind, the man's voice vibrated with the sound of money.

'Good evening,' Jordan replied amiably enough, still, Chloe felt his frustration hum through his fingertips as his hand tightened on hers. Courtesy demanded they stop. 'Chloe, I'd like you to meet Wes and Sybil Hampton.'

She waited for more from Jordan; something that might indicate who she was and what she meant to him. Some kind of acknowledgement at least.

Nothing. Not a word. Pain cramped her whole body. She withdrew her hand from his—or maybe he let her go—and nodded at the couple with a murmured, 'It's nice to meet you.'

Wes said something about being pleased to meet her too and Sybil gave her a brief condescending smile and maybe she even spoke, but Chloe barely heard over the rushing noise in her ears. Because Jordan couldn't have made it clearer that he didn't want to be seen here with her.

The way Stewart had reacted when they'd bumped into friends on that last day.

'Fancy running into you again so soon after the ball,' Sybil gushed, touching Jordan's arm, her rings flashing in the street light, Chloe forgotten. 'We're just on our way to meet the Brodericks for a light supper, if you'd like to join us...' She trailed off, looking at Chloe, who was clearly *not* invited.

'Not tonight, Sybil.'

'Tomorrow, then. We're touring a few wineries—it's not too late to add an extra. The limo's booked for nine a.m. Wanda's coming and she's been dying to catch up with you. I was only saying the other day th—'

'Thanks, but I'm going to be busy,' he said, edging away.

Her face creased with disappointment and she cast a telling glance at Chloe. 'Well. Another time, then.'

'Come on, Sybil,' Wes muttered, nodding at Jordan as he prodded his wife forward. 'Let the man and his lady friend go.'

Lady friend in her uniform and work shoes. Way out of Jordan's league and the Hamptons knew it. She could only be with him for one reason. Sex.

The interaction was enough time for Chloe to shake off the momentary insanity that had taken hold for a few unguarded moments. Insanity that would truly be her undoing if she succumbed to it.

As the couple walked off, Jordan reached for Chloe's hand again, but she moved out of his way and stopped. 'I'm not coming home with you, Jordan.'

His expression remained passive but there was a flash of... something...in his eyes. 'Why not?'

'I need to go.'

'We'll go to yours, then.'

'No. I mean I need to move on. With my life. I've been in Melbourne too long.'

He studied her a moment, then shook his head. 'That's not what you're really saying, is it.' Not a question.

She lifted her chin anyway. 'Who are you to tell me what I'm saying?'

'I'm someone who cares,' he said quietly. 'Someone who knows you better than you think.'

Care wasn't love, and it wasn't enough—not from Jordan. She shook her head. 'I'm going to Sydney. Catch up with my family.'

'Great—I hope you enjoy the family reunion but I'm not buying your story this time, Chloe.'

'It's not a story,' she said desperately.

His gaze narrowed. 'You're afraid to be with me.'

'Those friends of yours—'

'They're not my friends, they're business acquaintances. However they do donate huge sums of money to my charity.'

'You didn't introduce me to them as anyone who meant something to you.'

He paused, looking nonplussed. 'I assumed you wanted to keep your anonymity. Sybil's a busybody with connections in high—'

'*No.*' She jabbed a finger in the air. 'You didn't know how to introduce me because I don't fit into your life like your other women. I'm a problem for you outside the bedroom. I'm not educated and wealthy like the people you associate with. I don't belong here. With you. In your world.'

'What the *hell* are you talking about?' His body radiated an impatient energy and he shoved his hands in his pockets and shifted to the balls of his feet so he appeared to loom over her. 'You'll never belong anywhere because you never stay long enough. For once in your life, stop running. You might find what you're looking for right here.'

The way he said it, the expression in his eyes, almost tempted her to believe. To hope. To take a chance…

'What are you saying, Jordan? That you're offering something permanent?'

She swore he paled beneath his tan, his eyes flashed *PANIC* in big blue letters and she had her answer. Any foolish dreams she might have had died right then and there on the footpath. 'I didn't think so.'

'Permanent's a big leap… I didn't m—'

'Enough.' She shot out a staying hand. 'Don't worry, Jordan, South America's next on my travel itinerary and *Carnaval* in Rio is only a few months away.' Lies, all lies. 'Thanks to your generosity. This time it'll be first class all the way.'

Was it possible to smile when your soul was dying? But she managed it as she backed away, committing his face to memory, etching his image on her heart. 'I'll send you a postcard.'

'Chloe—'

'*Don't* follow me.' She turned around and began to walk. She knew he'd respect her wishes because she remembered the first night they'd met when she'd asked the same of him.

This time it was different. This time she was leaving her heart with him.

The next few days went by in a blur. She was truly sorry to tell Dana she was leaving with almost no notice—Chloe had never left a boss in the lurch that way. But not nearly as sorry as she was to be leaving Jordan without the right and final words being said between them. Dana said she understood Chloe's decision but made her promise to keep in touch and leave her contact details.

It didn't take much time for Chloe to pack her stuff and organise to relocate it to Sydney. She rode her scooter interstate, keeping at a leisurely pace and stopping twice overnight in little country towns.

When she arrived in Sydney, she found a clean, comfortable motel only forty minutes' drive from her childhood home and adjacent to a park. It gave her time to think.

Jordan had said something that last time that she could not get out of her head: *You'll never belong anywhere because you never stay long enough. For once in your life, stop running. You might find what you're looking for...*

True words, she realised, now. Every one.

With him, no matter how short their time had been, she'd learned how it felt to belong with someone. She'd realised he'd been protecting her, not embarrassed by her. That when their fling was over, he was assuring her privacy by not revealing their past to the rest of the world. No one would ever call her Jordan's ex-lover. He'd always accepted her as she was and never tried to change her.

It had taken Jordan to show her that running away wasn't an answer. The big *P* word had scared him, no denying it, yet she'd run before giving him a chance to respond.

Left him before he could leave her.

And who could say how things might have ended? How it might have gone if she'd stayed and had a conversation about it?

So instead of renting, she put down roots for the first time in her life and bought a little Victorian terrace home in Paddington that was unoccupied and available immediately. *A renovator's dream,* according to the ad. She spent the next couple of weeks keeping busy and focused on choosing furniture and fabrics, cushions and crockery.

Signing up for a three-year counselling course online that was starting in three months was thrilling and scary but that was a challenge she was confident she'd meet.

Meanwhile, exchanging regular emails with her family who still didn't know she was back in Australia gave her time to plan how to re-establish those ties without letting them walk all over her.

But every night when she lay alone beneath her feather quilt, other thoughts and images tumbled through her head like a noisy street parade. Then she'd climb from her bed and sit for hours by the quaint glass doors that opened onto her narrow balcony with its panoramic view of old tin roofs and iron lace. By fate or coincidence, it faced south-west, so whichever city Jordan was in Chloe imagined him there. She also imagined having the guts to walk into his office and finally tell him what was in her heart and why she could never be with him.

* * *

In his Melbourne apartment, Jordan lay on his bed staring at the darkened ceiling. Nearly midnight. He supposed he should fix something to eat or even rouse himself enough to go out and grab some takeaway but his appetite was non-existent.

Who knew a month could pass so slowly? Or that he'd be such disgustingly bad company? Finally tonight Dana had told him not to turn up at her place until he'd made a decision. Yep, Jordan Blackstone, who prided himself on his decision-making skills.

The man who also prided himself on his ability to control his circumstances and never allowed emotions to interfere with his life.

That man was history. He barked out a harsh laugh that seemed to echo back at him in the stillness. Yeah, a joke.

A woman had brought him to this. A tiny woman with mussed blonde hair and a smile that could tempt any man to lean in for just one taste.

Which was exactly how he'd got himself into this situation.

But unlike other women he'd known, Chloe had never tried to manipulate him. She might have fallen into his lap but she hadn't fallen at his feet. A willing listener and friend, even when he'd pushed her away.

She wasn't after fame or fortune. He'd discovered earlier today that an anonymous donation had been made to Rapper One. The exact same amount he'd deposited into Chloe's account the night they'd returned to Australia. She'd donated her second instalment to his charity.

Money truly wasn't important to her. She was proudly independent with a sense of humour and adventure. She'd accepted him for who he was, not what he could do for her.

She also had a vulnerable side she worked damn hard to hide by feigning carelessness and not sticking around—for fear of being left. A front, a mask. She'd never told him wh the man she'd loved had left her—and he was certain he'd left her and not the other way around—but clearly the scum was the reason she was always moving on.

Switching on his bedside light, he studied the paper Dana had given him again. Chloe's address. An inner Sydney suburb. For how long? he wondered. How long would it be before the adventurer in her beckoned and she took off for places unknown?

And the next time he might never find her.

The thought struck out of nowhere with the speed and devastation of a lightning bolt. He sat up so fast he knocked the lamp to the floor with a crash of broken glass, plunging him into darkness.

He barely noticed. Urgency was pounding through his system, stabbing through his brain until all focus narrowed to a single pinpoint, one thought.

He couldn't lose her.

He *wouldn't* lose her.

He would *not* lose the woman he loved.

Hang on... *Love?* Every muscle in his body tightened. Every fibre, every sinew, vibrated as if he'd been tuned in to some great musical humming through the universe. His skin prickled, he heard his pulse drumming in his ears, the blood pumping through his heart. He didn't know what to do with the energy so he sprang up off the bed and paced to the living room. Yes, he realised on a burst of something that felt like relief mingled with surprise—he loved Chloe, and he'd never felt so intense, so energised, so alive.

He'd always thought love made a man weak and yet he'd never felt so strong.

Strong enough to toss away his flawed and outdated ideas and reach out for something he'd never known he'd wanted until now.

He snatched up his phone. It was only a little after ten in

Perth and he paid Roma an exorbitant income to be available at odd hours.

He had much to consider and decisions to make. Urgently. Then he needed to put those decisions into action....

CHAPTER FIFTEEN

Two days later

'HERE GOES…' CHLOE said, smoothing her paintbrush on the wall and watching the happy yellow colour slowly hide the drab beige beneath, transforming her kitchen into a sunny room where she could teach herself to cook and grow herbs. *Her* kitchen. She smiled and jiggled her hips to the rock'n'roll party happening on her tinny radio on the window sill alongside her first pot of parsley.

She dipped her brush again, working rhythmically while she sang along and considered new possibilities. She could raise hens. Or ducks. Or get a cat. Now she'd committed to staying in one place for a while, a whole new world had opened up to her.

There was just one vital part missing in that world…

No—there he was again. In her head. In her heart. And she must let him go because she knew now she'd never fit in his world. This time she slapped her brush against the wall and felt its resulting cool, thick splash on her brow. She swiped it away with her forearm. She needed to get this place in shape so that she could invite her family over and show them she could be the person they wanted her to be. *Correction, Chloe.* The person *she* wanted to be.

Because being the person she wanted to be would surely

impact on others she came into contact with in a positive way. Confident in herself and her abilities, wholly focused, steady and reliable. Constant. Jordan had taught her how to bring out those qualities she'd not realised she had.

The call she'd made this morning had been the hardest she'd ever made, but worth it. The familiar sound of Mum's voice had brought so many emotions to the surface, she'd been tempted to tell her she could be there in forty minutes, but she needed to stick to her plan, no matter how hard, and take things slow for the next couple of weeks.

They'd talked for an hour. About the man who'd made it possible for Chloe to help out financially. About the prejudiced SOB who'd humiliated her. About the one who'd ripped her off. Both women had voiced regrets but Chloe spoke firmly about how she wanted things to be from now on.

Filled with new hope, she smiled, tempted to paint a rainbow arc across the wall with her little pots of trial colours. And why not?

The sound of a car pulling up outside had her glancing across the living space to the sitting-room window. Through the faded lacy scrim she could see a hulking black four-wheel drive with dull and dented bodywork that indicated it had endured its fair share of off-road adventures.

The driver climbed out, staring at her place behind mirrored sunglasses, and everything inside her stilled. The kind of tall, dark, broad-shouldered male who could send shivers down her spine just by being alive. Her heart bounded into her chest. Only one man could do that…

The paintbrush slid from her grasp and landed on the tarp she'd spread over the scarred timber floor. *Dana, I'm going to kill you.* She watched, frozen, as he trotted up her worn stone steps, then reared back when he disappeared from view and rang the little antique iron bell she'd painted blue and hung beside the door.

'Chloe,' she heard him say and he rang the bell again. When she still couldn't move, he tapped on the door and said, 'I know you're there, Chloe, and I know you can hear me. I've come a long way and I'm not leaving until you see me, so answer the door. I just want to talk, so...'

So she pulled the door open and there he was and her heart raced and turned and tumbled over in her chest. Because he looked as if he'd done the ten-hour drive from Melbourne in seven and without a break. His face was shadow-stubbled, his shirt rumpled. And his eyes...they were bleary and bloodshot but there was also a clarity and resolution and maybe even a glimpse of something like fear that she'd never seen before and it had her heart tumbling some more.

'Hello, Blondie.'

'*How* did you know I could hear you?' she demanded without a greeting and hanging on to the door for support.

He shrugged. 'Took a chance. Can I come in?'

Oh, she missed that voice...but right now it sounded raspy and raw. 'I think you'd better.' She pulled the door wider. 'You look...awful.'

One eyebrow lifted. 'And you look gorgeous.' His grin was lazy. Tired. The grin that always made her heart race.

Her mind awhirl, she gestured him inside. 'Um...excuse the mess. I'm renovating.'

'*Renovating?*' His eyes widened in surprise, then he nodded. 'So that's what the splotch is.' He raised a hand toward her brow, then let it drop and moved back as if he'd overstepped some boundary.

'I wasn't expecting...visitors.' She glanced down at the paint-stained man's flannel shirt she'd thrown on over her leggings and wanted to groan. 'I'll just go and—'

'Don't go.' His gaze captured hers. 'I just want to look at you a moment. You're a balm for tired eyes.'

She tore her gaze away. 'At least let me take off this paint shirt.' Peeling it off her arms, she let it fall to the floor. 'Better,' she murmured, then frowned down at herself. 'Or maybe not.'

Jordan's fatigue-blurred vision still delighted in the sight of Chloe in leggings and an oversized shirt that reminded him of that faded T-shirt—the one she'd worn in Dubai the night she'd waited up for him when things hadn't looked good for the mine. 'You look beautiful whatever you're wearing— oversize paint shirt or too-small rhinestone-covered costume.'

She paused at mention of that but didn't look at him, heading towards a tiny kitchen cluttered with paint pots and rags and smelling of turpentine. 'You should get some sleep— obviously your sight's impaired,' she said as she walked. 'I'll make you a warm drink—what do you want?'

You. Only you. 'Whatever's handy.'

'Herbal tea, then.'

'Fine.'

She cleared a space at a little round table, told him to have a seat, then fussed with the makings of the tea. The beat of an Aussie band on the radio masked the lack of conversation.

He waited until she set two cups of camomile tea on the table but she remained standing, twisting her fingers together and smelling of paint and perfume. 'Sit down, Chloe.' He leaned across and pulled out the chair next to him. 'We need to talk.'

She took the chair opposite instead. 'Yes.'

He sipped his tea thirstily to wet his dust-dry mouth before resting his arms on the table and looking into her eyes. 'First off, I've been giving a lot of thought to why you ran away that last night. And when I say a lot of thought, I've thought of nothing else. Nothing. My work's suffered and my PA's probably going to quit unless I start being human again.

'I'm sorry,' she said, her gaze darting away. 'I didn't mean for that to happen.'

'You accused me of something I didn't understand. Still don't understand.'

'I know. And I'm sorry for that too.'

'Amongst other things—which I'll get to directly—you said you couldn't live in my world because you didn't belong.' He saw the pain in her eyes and wanted to reach out but didn't know whether she'd welcome it. 'Help me understand that, Chloe.'

She sighed, spread her hands on the table and studied them rather than look at him. 'Remember the dragon you slayed for me in our desert honeymoon? Well, seems he's not quite dead after all.'

Jordan's eyes narrowed. 'What the hell…?'

'No, no, nothing like that. I've never seen him again.' She blew out a breath and fixed her eyes on Jordan's. 'Okay, it was like this. We spent our time together in his home with his son. And that was fine—I was happy with that because I loved Brad too. But he never took me out unless it was to a private booth in an out-of-the-way restaurant. I never met his friends. Until one night when we bumped into a couple accidentally.'

A picture was forming in Jordan's mind and making a lot of sense. 'Like when we bumped into Wes and Sybil.'

'Exactly like that. When we got home he told me it was over. I was devastated, and tried to discuss it. Long story short, he accused me of sexual harassment, made sure I couldn't get a job with any nanny service in the UK. They wouldn't take my word over his. He *used* me. Which is why I was so angry and upset with you that first night when you accused me of coming on to you.'

The blood simmered hot and dark through Jordan's veins. 'You should've told me. I would've understood, but you ran away.'

Chloe realised that now. Her pulse sped up. Was it too

late? 'You told me to stop running and I asked if you were talking about something permanent and I've never seen a guy so panicked.'

'You caught me by surprise. You didn't give me time.'

'Well, I took your advice about running and bought this place. It's mine. All mine. And I'm not going anywhere.' She lifted her chin. 'I'm going to raise chickens.'

He smiled slowly. 'Can I tell you a story?'

She didn't answer straight away. 'Depends. Does it have a happy ending?'

'I hope so.' He leaned closer, so that she could smell the road and travel dust on his skin.

She nodded. 'All good stories start with "once upon a time".'

He smiled, the light in his eyes reminding her of springtime and new beginnings. 'Okay. *Once upon a time*, there was a guy called Jordan who was locked in a tower. A prison of his own making, because he couldn't see beyond his work and his meaningless relationships, and he thought he was content. He had no desire to escape until a girl called Blondie who lived for adventure, fell into his lap. She was beautiful and kind and clever and he realised he'd be missing out on something amazing if he didn't make this girl his.'

Make her his? Her heart stopped beating. Literally stopped. And swelled. And sang.

'But now he's not sure she'll have him because it took him so long to realise he loves her and he's not even sure whether she loves him back.'

Tears welled up into her eyes. 'Oh, J—'

When she would have touched him, when she would have wept with joy and flung herself at him, he held up a hand. 'Let me finish.'

He paused, then said, 'So he wants adventurous Blondie to come on an adventure with him to explore what they have

He's packed enough gear into his well-used off-road vehicle for the two of them for a few weeks. Or months. However long and however far she wants to go. He wants to take her into gold-mining country because he knows a thing or two about it. He wants to teach her a new skill—how to pan for gold during the day and…well, he has other things he'd like to teach her at night, under the stars.'

She drew a few stunned breaths while she processed everything. 'What about his work? They can't roam the gold-fields forever. Where will they live? Blondie just bought a house.'

'He's organised to have time off. He's not taken leave since he took over the company so he figures he's entitled. As for living arrangements, Jordan has responsibilities in Perth and Melbourne but he's been thinking of opening up a branch in Sydney. There's no reason why they can't spend time in each place. As long as they're together. As long as she loves him back. He thinks—'

'Blondie's pretty sure she agrees. She does know she's definite about loving him back. Enough talk.' Chloe scraped back her chair, plonked her butt on his lap and pressed her mouth to his to shut him up.

And he tasted so good—dark and rich and *hers*.

Then he hauled her against his chest and carried her to bed and they spent the next little while making warm slow love and not talking at all.

Hours later, when they woke and the evening sky was turning yellow, he reached for his discarded jeans and pulled a small square box out of the pocket. '*Now* will you wear this?' He flipped it open and the familiar little gold ring glinted on a bed of blue velvet.

'It's a wedding ring,' Chloe said, staring at it, remembering all the adventures they'd had while she was Mrs Jordan Blackstone. 'We're not married.'

'Do you want to be?'

'I always thought I couldn't do marriage but I know now that it was because I was afraid. But with you—you give me the courage to give it a try.'

She looked up to see the sun shining in his eyes. 'What about you? You told me you're not a marrying man.'

'I didn't think I was. Until I found you.'

'But you nearly married Lynette.'

The sun slid behind a cloud and his eyes sombred. 'A manipulator. A liar. A gold-digger. And I was a fool.'

'No. You were never a fool.' Chloe rested her chin on his chest but didn't take the ring. Not yet. 'Will you tell me what happened now, since I've come clean with you?'

The corners of his mouth turned down as if he didn't want to talk but needed to. 'She was attractive, outgoing and intelligent and soon after we met I asked her to be my date at my annual charity ball. She showed a keen interest in the kids I was working with and it wasn't long before she was talking about how if she had a house she'd do it up and provide a place-slash-time out for troubled kids blah, blah, blah.

'Meanwhile, we were falling in love—at least I was. Or thought I was. So when she hinted several times that if we were married, we could foster kids in our own home, I fell for it. I understood those neglected kids because I'd been one of them. Not quite the same but even a rich kid knows how it feels to be unwanted.'

'Your childhood wasn't good…'

'Ina never wanted kids. When I was born she refused to have any more, then as soon as she could she shipped me off to boarding school. On school holidays Dad used to take me out into the bush gold-panning. I loved those times.'

He shook his head as if he wanted to rid himself of the memories. Remembering Dana's advice about him loathing sympathy, Chloe remained still and waited for him to continue.

'Anyway, I owned a place in the city I'd been thinking of selling but I gifted it to Lynette as a wedding surprise the week before. I stupidly put it in her name.

'We were due to get married in Las Vegas. She told me she had a last-minute errand to run before we flew out but she never turned up at the airport. She'd sold the house already and disappeared. I never saw her again.'

'You didn't try to find her? Get something back?'

'I suppose I could have, but why would I expose myself for the idiot that I was? Even Foolish Freddy wouldn't try to find her. That's an end to it, Chloe. I don't ever want to talk about her again.'

'Thank you for telling me. Let's make a deal to not talk about our past again.'

'Done.' His stomach grumbled at that moment, and, glad for the opportunity to change topics, she smoothed her palm over his lean, hard torso. 'Hungry?'

He covered her hand and brought it to his lips for a nibble. 'Since I haven't eaten since I left Melbourne, yes.'

'Gosh, when was that?'

'It was dark, that's all I remember. Chloe.' He slid the gold band onto the finger on her right hand and eased it over the knuckle. A tight fit but manageable. 'Wear your ring on this hand until we get married. Whenever that might be—a month from now or a year—up to you. But I want to see my gold there and know we're partners. That we've made a promise. A commitment. That you're prepared to take on the biggest challenge of your life.'

She smiled at that man she loved through misty eyes. 'It's a deal. And now we've made that promise…how does Christmas sound?'

Jordan felt a grin break out on his face, a relief after the tension he'd endured since he'd made his decision. 'It sounds amazing. Like you.' He breathed in the scent of her hair and let it out on a sigh of contentment. Home. He was finally home. 'Do you want the big event or the register office?'

'I don't care, but do know I want my family there when we do it.'

That knowledge pleased him immensely. For all her adventures, he knew she missed them, that she needed that bond of family. 'So have you seen them yet?'

'I was waiting till I got this place fixed up…' She shook her head. 'I know I said I was up for any challenge, but, even though I've talked to Mum and we understand each other better now, I'm still a bit scared of actually facing up to them.'

He reached for her hand, his fingers sliding over the ring of golden promise. 'We'll go face them together.'

'We will?'

'Of course we will. We're partners, a team. And they're my future in-laws. I'm looking forward to being part of a family again.'

Chloe rested her chin on his chest, looked into the cerulean-blue depths of his eyes and saw forever. 'Partners. Pookie and Blondie.'

He nodded, those eyes crinkling up at the edges. 'And they lived happily ever after.'

* * * * *

A sneaky peek at next month...

MODERN™

INTERNATIONAL AFFAIRS, SEDUCTION & PASSION GUARANTEED

My wish list for next month's titles...

In stores from 19th April 2013:

☐ A Rich Man's Whim – Lynne Graham

☐ A Touch of Notoriety – Carole Mortimer

☐ Maid for Montero – Kim Lawrence

☐ Captive in his Castle – Chantelle Shaw

☐ Heir to a Dark Inheritance – Maisey Yates

In stores from 3rd May 2013:

☐ A Price Worth Paying? – Trish Morey

☐ The Secret Casella Baby – Cathy Williams

☐ Strictly Temporary – Robyn Grady

☐ Her Deal with the Devil – Nicola Marsh

Available at WHSmith, Tesco, Asda, Eason, Amazon and Apple

Just can't wait?

Visit us Online

You can buy our books online a month before they hit the shops! **www.millsandboon.co.uk**

0413/01

Special Offers

Every month we put together collections and longer reads written by your favourite authors.

Here are some of next month's highlights— and don't miss our fabulous discount online!

 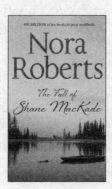 

On sale 19th April　　On sale 3rd May　　On sale 3rd May

Save 20% on all Special Releases

2 Free Books!

Join the Mills & Boon Book Club

Want to read more **Modern**™ books? We're offering you **2 more** absolutely **FREE!**

We'll also treat you to these fabulous extras:

- **Books up to 2 months ahead of shops**
- **FREE home delivery**
- **Bonus books with our special rewards scheme**
- **Exclusive offers and much more!**

Get your free books now!

Visit us Online

Find out more at
www.millsandboon.co.uk/freebookoffer

The World of Mills & Boon®

There's a Mills & Boon® series that's perfect for you. We publish ten series and, with new titles every month, you never have to wait long for your favourite to come along.

Blaze®
Scorching hot, sexy reads
4 new stories every month

By Request
Relive the romance with the best of the best
9 new stories every month

Cherish™
Romance to melt the heart every time
12 new stories every month

Desire™
Passionate and dramatic love stories
8 new stories every month